PRAISE FOR
#1 NEW YORK TIM
BARB~~

MW00613822

"I love *The Callaways*! Heartwarming romance, intriguing suspense and sexy alpha heroes. What more could you want?"
-- *NYT Bestselling Author* **Bella Andre**

"I adore *The Callaways*, a family we'd all love to have. Each new book is a deft combination of emotion, suspense and family dynamics. A remarkable, compelling series!"
-- *USA Today Bestselling Author* **Barbara O'Neal**

"Once I start reading a Callaway novel, I can't put it down. Fast-paced action, a poignant love story and a tantalizing mystery in every book!"
-- *USA Today Bestselling Author* **Christie Ridgway**

"In the tradition of LaVyrle Spencer, gifted author Barbara Freethy creates an irresistible tale of family secrets, riveting adventure and heart-touching romance."
-- *NYT Bestselling Author* **Susan Wiggs**
on Summer Secrets

"This book has it all: heart, community, and characters who will remain with you long after the book has ended. A wonderful story."
-- *NYT Bestselling Author* **Debbie Macomber**
on Suddenly One Summer

"Freethy has a gift for creating complex characters."
-- ***Library Journal***

"Barbara Freethy is a master storyteller with a gift for spinning tales about ordinary people in extraordinary situations and drawing readers into their lives."

"Freethy's skillful plotting and gift for creating sympathetic characters will ensure that few dry eyes will be left at the end of the story."

"Freethy skillfully keeps the reader on the hook, and her tantalizing and believable tale has it all-- romance, adventure, and mystery."

"Freethy's story-telling ability is top-notch."

"Powerful and absorbing...sheer hold-your-breath suspense."

"A page-turner that engages your mind while it tugs at your heartstrings...Don't Say A Word has made me a Barbara Freethy fan for life!"

Also By Barbara Freethy

Bachelors and Bridesmaids
#1 Kiss Me Forever
#2 Steal My Heart
#3 All Your Loving
#4 Before I Do
#5 Falling Into You
#6 Forever Starts Tonight *Coming Soon!*

The Callaway Series
On A Night Like This (#1)
So This Is Love (#2)
Falling For A Stranger (#3)
Between Now and Forever (#4)
Nobody But You (Callaway Wedding Novella)
All A Heart Needs (#5)
That Summer Night (#6)
When Shadows Fall (#7)
Somewhere Only We Know (#8)
If I Didn't Know Better (#9)
Tender is the Night (#10) *Coming soon!*

Lightning Strikes Trilogy
Beautiful Storm (#1)
Lightning Lingers (#2) *Coming soon!*
Summer Rain (#3) *Coming soon!*

FALLING INTO YOU

Bridesmaids and Batchelors #5

BARBARA FREETHY

HYDE
STREET
PRESS

HYDE STREET PRESS
Published by Hyde Street Press
1325 Howard Avenue, #321, Burlingame, California 94010

Printed in the United States of America

Cover design by Damonza.com

ISBN: 9781-9-437811-2-6

Chapter One

He was the kind of man her father would have shot on sight—faded jeans that hung low on his hips, a dark t-shirt under a black leather jacket, wavy brown hair that drifted past the collar of his jacket, a day's growth of beard on his face and a wicked smile in his dark brown eyes.

Maggie Gordon smiled to herself as she watched the man walk the length of the luxurious lobby. He knew he was being watched. He'd probably known it since he'd roared up in front of Napa Valley's prestigious Stratton Hotel on his motorcycle and casually deposited it with the valet. Judging by the swagger of his walk, he didn't give a damn what anyone thought.

He was a lucky guy not to have to follow the rules or worry about the opinion of others. Maggie had never had that kind of freedom, not with an Army general for a father, and certainly not with a rigid boss like Harry Stone.

The thought of her manager made her stand up straighter, and the grin that was lurking at the corners of her mouth vanished. She could not afford to lose her job, not after the last six years of saving every dollar from every paycheck in order to be able to buy a house of her own one day. Now, she was so close to having her dream come true, she could taste it.

The man's booted heels clicked against the marble floor as he came to a halt in front of the desk. He set his black duffel bag down on the floor, casting one sweeping look around the lobby, obviously amused by the attention he was drawing from a group of older women by the elevator. While Maggie quite approved of his rugged, sexy appearance, the women in town for a convention regarded him with disdain, as if he'd just dragged some dirt into the hotel.

The man directed his gaze at her, a smile lurking in his eyes.

"May I help you?" Maggie asked, pleased by the cool tone of her voice. It was a nice contrast to the unexpected heat surging through her body. It had been awhile since she'd felt such a jolt of attraction.

The man gave her a long look, and then said, "Kathy?"

She looked at him in surprise. "What? I'm not—"

"I've missed you, baby. Come here and give me a kiss."

Before she could say she wasn't Kathy, he reached across the counter and grabbed her by the shoulder. She had no time to do anything but open her mouth, which was a definite mistake. His kiss was hot and hungry, his tongue sliding inside her mouth, bringing a wave of heat along with it.

"Miss Gordon!" Harry Stone's shocked voice brought her to her senses.

She immediately pulled away, blinking somewhat dazedly at the handsome stranger who'd just kissed the breath out of her.

"What is going on here?" her manager demanded, his homely, round face turning red with anger as he moved down the counter.

Maggie's hand flew to her mouth, her lips still tingling from the impact of his kiss. "I—I—" She looked at her boss in confusion and then back at the man who had started it all.

He grinned, no trace of remorse in his eyes. Instead, there was a sparkle and the lingering gleam of passion, which only made her feel more unsettled. It was time to regain control of the situation.

"Why did you do that?" she demanded.

"I thought you were someone else. My mistake." He cocked his head to the right as he studied her face. "I guess you don't look much like her after all, and you sure as hell don't kiss like her."

Maggie frowned at what sounded like a negative comparison, but as her manager cleared his throat again, she realized this stranger's opinion of her was the least of her problems.

"Do you have a reservation?" she asked, getting back to business.

"Cole Hastings."

She put his name into the computer. "How do you want to pay for this?"

He pushed a credit card across the counter. She ran the card and then completed the check-in while Harry Stone watched her every move.

"Room 316 would be a better choice," Harry said as the assigned room number appeared on the screen.

She cast him a quick look. Room 316 was on the street side and over the garbage area. It was the worst room in the hotel. "We have an opening on the fourth floor," she replied in a hushed voice.

"No, that one is reserved." He reached over her and punched the buttons to change the room number. Maggie had no choice but to hand Mr. Hastings a key and hope he wouldn't come to her to complain.

Cole sent her a thoughtful glance and then signed the bill without comment.

"Enjoy your stay," Maggie said politely, adding silently that she hoped it would be shorter than the ten days he had registered for.

"It's off to a good start," he said with a wicked smile. Then he picked up his duffel bag, swung it over one shoulder and sauntered toward the elevator.

Maggie took in a deep breath and let it out slowly. Her heart was still pounding against her ribs, her pulse racing faster than it did during her workouts. What on earth was the matter with her? You'd think she'd never been kissed before. Although, she'd never been kissed quite like that. Whoever Kathy was—she was a lucky woman.

"Your behavior was unprofessional," Harry said, drawing her attention back to him. His face was lined with irritation. "You're treading on thin ice, Miss Gordon. You continue to get involved with our guests in a manner that goes beyond your duties."

"Mr. Stone, please. I do not know why that man kissed me. I did nothing to encourage him. You heard him. He mistook me for someone else."

He looked at her in obvious disbelief. "I've been working in the hotel business for over fifteen years, and I've never seen that happen before."

"There's a first time for everything."

Her comment only heightened his anger. "Your

attitude is not appreciated. This incident will go in your file, which I'll be reviewing with Mrs. Stratton next month. Any more events like this, and you'll be looking for another job."

"It will never happen again. I love this job. I need it." It went against the grain to beg, but she couldn't let him kill her dream because of a stranger's mistake.

"Then do your job quietly and efficiently. This is a luxury hotel. We are courteous, helpful and above all, discreet. Understood?"

"Yes, sir."

"I have to go out for an hour. Try not to get into any more trouble before dinner."

Maggie nodded, breathing a sigh of relief as her manager left the reception area. Harry Stone had always been hard and rigid but in the last two months he'd become quite antagonistic toward her, and she didn't really understand why.

"You certainly liven this place up." Karen Monte, a tall, slim blonde, walked around the counter and slipped her purse into a desk drawer as she returned from lunch.

"What did you see?"

"Everything. Who was the hot guy you were kissing?"

"He was kissing me. And I don't know who he was. He just reached across the counter and grabbed me. He called me Kathy. It was the strangest thing. He said he thought I was someone else."

Karen shook her head in amazement. "Why don't things like that ever happen to me? The most attention I got today was when a foreign tour group asked me to be in their holiday photograph." She paused, taking a quick glance around the lobby, but most of the interested onlookers were now going about their own business. "So, how was the kiss?"

"How was it?" Maggie echoed. "It was—" She shrugged her shoulders, trying to think of an adequate description, like wonderful or fantastic or unbelievable. No, those words weren't right at all. "It doesn't matter how it was; he almost got me fired. I should have slapped his face."

"Really? Because if a man who looked like that kissed me, I'd be more interested in kissing him back."

"That man is trouble. I hope I never see him again." Maggie turned away from Karen and self-consciously touched her fingers to her tingling lips.

Cole Hastings had turned her world upside down with thirty seconds of heat. She had gotten a taste of that elusive something she had always wondered about, and it had to come from the absolutely wrong man. Cole kissed like an outlaw, and she was looking for a good guy this time around. She'd tried reforming a bad boy once before; she wouldn't do it again.

Cole stretched out on the bed, raising his arms over his head and letting the tension unwind from his stiff muscles. So much for the freedom of a motorcycle; he felt as if he'd been on horseback for three days straight. Muscles he didn't even know he had were aching.

Still, it was a good ache. Physical exertion and the pain of exercise had helped block out the emotional pain for over two years now. He could hardly believe it had been that long.

He closed his eyes, thinking about the happy oblivion

of sleep. But instead of seeing the welcoming cocoon of darkness, he saw a cloud of strawberry blonde hair, light blue eyes and a soft, open mouth. He smiled to himself. The look on her face had been priceless.

He had kissed her for a lark. She had look so damned straitlaced in her navy blue skirt and button-down blouse. He had wanted to shake her up, and he had. Unfortunately, he'd also shaken himself up.

So, go to sleep, he told himself, but her face kept floating in front of his eyes, and he absentmindedly rubbed the back of his hand across his mouth.

Her kiss had been more than he bargained for. He had expected her to yank away, not kiss him back with such warm, spontaneous generosity.

The hotel phone rang, and he opened his eyes with a groan. Although he wanted to think the beautiful hotel clerk was reaching out, he had a feeling he knew exactly who was on the line. He lifted the receiver. "Yeah?"

"Is that the way your mother taught you to answer the phone?" The woman's voice was sharp and stern and brought a smile to his lips.

"Aunt Ida. You must have ESP. I just checked in."

"Not ESP, just an ear to the ground. You caused quite a stir in my lobby. How are you, dear?"

He yawned. "Tired. I drove up from LA today. It was quite a ride." He stuffed a pillow more comfortably under his head, knowing his aunt's penchant for long conversations.

"You're not still driving that motorcycle, are you?"

"Yes. It suits me. I'm a rambling man these days. You know that."

"I do, and some days I'd like to join you on the back of that bike."

The sparkle in her voice made him smile at the thought of his seventy-year-old aunt hanging onto his waist as they careened around a corner. The rest of the family would be horrified, but she would probably love it.

"I'm dying to see you, honey," Ida continued. "I want to talk about the hotel and some other things."

"What other things?" He sat up, knowing he better have his wits about him, or Ida would talk him into something he didn't want to do. She was very difficult to say no to. "I told you I'd come up here to see you and check out your operation, but nothing long-term. You understand that, don't you? I'm leaving in ten days."

"Of course you are."

"Aunt Ida," he said warningly. "Don't get any ideas about pulling me deeper into the family business. I like being the occasional troubleshooter. I get to travel all over the country and never see the same people twice, but that's it."

"Some people are worth seeing twice, but I'm not going to push. I do, however, insist that we have some fun while you're here. Although, I think you may have started without me. Did you really kiss my front desk clerk?"

Cole smiled. "Guilty."

"You're a bad boy."

"And I've been punished with the worst room in the hotel." Cole looked around as he spoke. He had a queen-sized bed and a decent-sized TV, but the room overlooked the garbage, which would be loud on pick-up day, and he suspected there were other hidden annoyances. After spending the past year traveling to each of the Stratton hotels and some of the hotels belonging to competing brands, he had a good idea where most hotel skeletons were hidden.

"I'm sorry about that," Ida continued. "Maybe next time you'll behave yourself. And why did you kiss Maggie? I thought you told me you weren't interested in women anymore."

"On a short-term basis they're okay."

There was a long silence, and Cole knew that Ida was an expert at reading between the lines. That's why he hadn't come to her hotel during the past few years. He'd preferred to talk to her on the phone or in email. Face-to-face, she would probably have more probing questions than he cared to answer. "Why don't I give you a call later?" he suggested. "I'm exhausted. I want to catch a nap."

"Of course. We'll have dinner. I know a wonderful restaurant that serves Thai food. You'll love it."

"Great. But I hope you chose a restaurant away from the hotel. We shouldn't be seen together."

"It's a little café miles away; it will be perfect. We can meet there. I'll text you the address."

"Really? You're into texting now?"

"I keep up," she said with a laugh.

"Great."

"Do you have any questions for me?"

He paused for one second too long.

"Her name is Maggie Gordon," Ida said. "Don't get any ideas about her."

"Why not? Is she married?"

"No, but she's so amazing that you wouldn't be able to leave her in ten days, and I know you don't want to change your plans."

Cole laughed. "You're waving a red flag right in my face. There's not a woman alive who could make me want to stay in one place—not ever again."

Ida sighed. "You remind me so much of myself."

"How so?"

"I used to think I knew everything, too."

Chapter Two

Maggie walked into the suite of offices behind the front desk at the end of her shift, surprised to find the hotel owner coming toward her. Ida Stratton was a beautiful older woman with stark white hair and sparkling blue eyes. Her long-sleeved blue knit dress and knee-high boots were both fun and sophisticated, which suited Ida quite well.

"Maggie, there you are. I was just coming to look for you."

"What can I do for you?" she asked, a little surprised that Mrs. Stratton would be looking for her. It was rare that the desk clerks spoke to the owner. In fact, Mr. Stone made sure everyone was very aware of the chain of command.

"Let's go outside." Ida tipped her head, directing Maggie's gaze toward the inner office where Harry Stone was conversing with one of the other employees. "I don't want to interrupt anyone's work."

"Of course," she said, aware of Mr. Stone giving her and Ida a speculative look as they left the offices. They walked out of the hotel and into the quietest of the three courtyards. In the center was a beautiful stone cupid astride a fountain that sprayed a jet of water against the blue and black tiles at its base. The flowers surrounding the courtyard were blooming gloriously in the late afternoon October sunshine.

Ida led her past a group of women playing bridge at one of the tables and they sat down on an oak bench by the fountain.

"This is my favorite spot," Ida said, taking a deep whiff of the floral-scented air. "I feel like I'm in my own garden instead of a courtyard surrounded by two hundred bedrooms."

"That's part of the charm of the Stratton. It feels a lot like home, or, in some cases, better than home."

Ida crossed her arms as the breeze lifted her hair. "Fall is definitely in the air."

"I'm ready. I love this time of the year."

"Me, too." Ida gave her a smile. "I have a favor to ask of you, Maggie."

"I'm happy to help."

"Good. I was hoping you would say that. My nephew is in town, and he's a wonderful boy, but I find I just don't have the energy to take him around and show him the sights." Ida sighed wearily. "My age is catching up with me, you know."

Maggie looked at her doubtfully, remembering two days earlier when she had seen her playing an active game of tennis with one of the resident pros.

"I hate to impose," Ida continued, "but I wonder if you could meet him for breakfast tomorrow and show him around downtown. I'll be tied up with the convention until the afternoon, and I really don't want him to be stuck in the hotel all morning. He'll be so bored and then he'll never come visit me again. Your shift doesn't start until three. I know it's a lot to ask, but I promise to return the favor."

Maggie thought of all the things she had planned for Saturday morning. But Mrs. Stratton rarely asked her for anything. How could she refuse such a simple request? Plus, she might need that favor one day.

"I'd be happy to compensate you for the time," Ida added.

"You don't have to do that. It's not a problem. I'd be happy to show your nephew around."

A smile spread across Ida's face. "That's wonderful. You're such a charming girl and always so friendly to everyone, I know he'll have fun with you. Why don't I drop him off at your house tomorrow morning around nine? Would that work? He's a sweet boy. I'm quite sure you'll like him."

"If he's anything like you, I'm positive I will."

"Good. How is everything else going?"

"It's great," she said, opting for the simplest answer. In truth, her life at the front desk had gotten worse and worse the past few months, but going against her boss would not get her anywhere.

"That's good to hear. I'll let you go then." As Ida stood up, she said, "Do you have a date tonight?"

"With my PJs and a good video."

"It's Friday night, dear. You should be getting romanced by some gorgeous man."

"I should be," she said with a laugh. "Unfortunately, there seem to be a lack of gorgeous men in my life."

"Well, you never know when that will change."

Thinking back to the crazy kiss she'd received earlier that day, she had to agree with Ida. "That's true. But I'm not worried about dating. It's all about work for me right now."

"Well, I appreciate your drive, dear, but a happy life should be filled with both work and play. Don't forget that."

"True." While she wasn't averse to playtime with a gorgeous man, she hadn't met anyone she really liked in a long time. She was beginning to wonder if she ever would. Five of her best friends had recently fallen in love and were now either married or engaged, so she was starting to feel the pressure of her late twenties. Her bridesmaid budget was also getting strained once again with the wedding of her friend Julie Michaels to Matt Kingsley in early December.

As she said good-bye to Mrs. Stratton and headed to the employee parking lot, her phone rang, and Julie's name flashed across the screen.

"Hi, Jules," she said, as she got into her car. "It's so weird; I was just thinking about you. How are the wedding plans going?"

"To be honest, they're a little overwhelming."

"Really?" She was surprised at the tension in Julie's voice. Julie was a fundraiser. She threw huge events all the time. A wedding should be a piece of cake. "What's going on?"

"Kate is going a little over the top with the wedding plans," Julie replied. "I hate to complain because she's doing everything for free, but this morning she told me she found this amazing horse and carriage she thinks I should ride away from the church in. Can you imagine me in a horse and carriage?"

Maggie laughed, thinking it was romantic, but didn't really fit the more practical Julie. "So tell her no."

"I tried. She said, 'just see it, you'll love it.'"

"Maybe you will love it."

"I don't think so. I want a small, intimate wedding, Maggie. Matt's professional life is so big. I want the wedding to feel personal. I want it to be just friends and family, the people who really matter to both of us."

That made sense. Matt Kingsley was the star player for the San Francisco Cougars baseball team, and fans often approached him and Julie for autographs and photographs. They rarely got through a restaurant meal without an interruption, and she couldn't imagine what it felt like to live in that kind of a fishbowl. But Julie had grown up in the world of pro baseball so at least she was familiar with the world.

"Don't worry, Jules. Your wedding will be perfect, and it will feel personal. We'll make sure of that. Do you want me to talk to Kate?"

"No, I just wanted to vent for a second. I'm fine. I'm happy to be marrying Matt, and I shouldn't be complaining."

"You're allowed. And you're certainly not the first bride to get a little tense. Liz was completely stressed out the month before her wedding. Just remember that it's not about the day; it's about the life you're going to have with Matt."

"I know. I never thought I could love a man this much," Julie said, her voice filled with emotion.

"He loves you, too. You should see the way he looks at you when you're not looking at him—like he's been in the desert for a long time, and you're a beautiful shimmering waterfall."

Julie laughed. "Okay, that was good."

"It was, wasn't it?"

"Thanks for cheering me up, Maggie. So, it looks like

the Cougars will be playing at home on Monday in the first game of the playoffs. I've reserved a box, and I want you to come. You're off on Mondays, right?"

"Yes, that sounds like fun."

"Good, Jessica is going to come, too. She's thinking of moving back to the Bay Area with Brandon. She wants to be closer to her family. I think it's really difficult being a single mom."

"I'm sure it is. It would be great if she were closer." Jessica had been living in San Diego the past several years and they only got to see her for the occasional weekend.

"It would be great if you were closer, too," Julie said pointedly. "Why do you have to live in Napa? There are luxury hotels in San Francisco."

"I like the Stratton and I love Napa. I'm not a city girl anymore. I like space around me. I like to be able to park in front of the drugstore."

"That is a luxury," Julie said with a laugh. "Anyway, I have to run. Matt and I are going to meet Isabella and Nick for dinner."

"That will be fun." Despite her defense of Napa, she did feel a little sad that she didn't get to see her friends as often as they saw each other. Not that she didn't have friends in Napa, but her group of college friends was special. They were the ones who knew her the best, who'd seen her at her best and at her worst and loved her unconditionally as she loved them.

"What are your plans tonight, Maggie?" Julie asked.

"It's been a long day, so I'm going to have a quiet night."

"You've been having too many of those lately. You're twenty-seven. You should be dating and dancing till dawn."

"Been there, done that—not all that exciting anymore."

"So there's no one new in your life?"

She hesitated, but couldn't stop herself from saying, "Well, a sexy stranger did walk into the hotel today and kissed the life out of me, so I guess that's new."

Julie gasped. "Seriously? Who? How? What?"

She laughed at the onslaught of questions. "He thought I was someone else."

"That sounds like a line."

"It does, doesn't it? I'm sure that's exactly what it was."

"Are you going to see him again?"

"He's staying at the hotel for the next week, so it's possible. But don't get too excited; he's not at all my type. He's a biker with long hair and a scruffy beard, and I'm betting there was at least one tattoo under the sleeves of his leather jacket."

"That sounds exactly like the type of guy you went after in college."

She winced at the reminder. "That was when I was young and stupid."

"And sad," Julie said quietly.

"That, too. But I learned my lesson. I stay away from bad boys now."

"What if they don't stay away from you?"

Julie's question sent a tingle down her spine. "I doubt he'll come looking for me. A man like that could have any woman he wanted."

"Except you, apparently. How was the kiss?"

"Pretty spectacular," she admitted. "What else would you expect from a sexy bad boy? I'm sure he's had lots of practice."

"Well, let me know if anything else happens."

"I will, but I wouldn't hold your breath."

"We'll talk soon. Love you, Mags."

"Love you, too," she said, as she ended the call.

She'd met Julie freshman year in college. Their dorm floor had provided the seven best friends of her life: the twins Andrea and Laurel, Julie and Liz, who'd grown up together, Isabella, Jessica, and Kate. Three of those women were already married and Julie and Isabella were engaged. She had a feeling she was going to be the last single woman standing in the not so distant future.

As she started the car and drove through the parking lot, she couldn't help glancing up at the third-floor hotel window where Cole Hastings was stashed in the worst room in the place. "No more bad boys," she muttered as she forced herself to look away.

—◦►◄◦—

Saturday morning, Cole stepped off the private elevator that led to his aunt's two-bedroom apartment on the top floor of the Stratton and knocked on the door. It was half past eight, and he was hungry and a little grumpy, which was often his usual state in the morning.

"Hello, honey," Ida said cheerfully as she opened the door. She stood on tiptoe to kiss his cheek. Then she shook a finger at him. "Did you forget to shave?"

"I didn't forget. This is the new me. It's part of my cover."

"I see. Well, come in. I have something to discuss with you."

Cole halted halfway through the door. "That sounds

ominous."

She laughed. "I thought you stopped worrying when you quit your big job."

"Good point."

Ida took his hand and pulled him over to the couch in her living room. "When we were talking last night, I got to thinking about how best to use your sharp eye, and I think I have a plan. I don't want Mr. Stone to know who you are or what you're doing here, at least not yet."

"That's not a problem. I can observe a lot without involving him."

"Yes, but observation today may be a problem and tomorrow as well. We're hosting a conservative women's convention this weekend, and there will be hundreds of lovely but very proper women in the hotel. I don't think you're going to fit in. I'd like you to disappear for the morning. We can meet back up around two for tea."

"All right. I can do that," he said warily, quite certain his aunt had more to say.

"Good. I'd love for you to take a look at the downtown area. You haven't been to Napa in years, and I'd love for you to get a better picture of the town and how we might enhance our hotel offerings to both locals and tourists."

"Fine. I'll hit the hot spots. But first, I'm going to grab breakfast in the café."

Ida grabbed his arm as he stood up. "The café is hosting breakfast for the convention."

"Then tell me where the nearest doughnut shop is, and I'll get out of your hair."

"One-twenty-five Paloma. I'll give you directions."

Cole's eyes narrowed. "You know the address to the doughnut shop?"

Ida laughed. "Of course not. I've arranged for you to meet one of my friends. She's going to have breakfast with you and show you the town. I want you to be polite. She's a very nice woman."

"You hooked me up with one of your lady friends?" He ran a hand through his hair. "Do I have to change and shave?"

"Only if you want to."

"I don't."

"Then go as you are. I don't want to make things difficult for you."

"Sure you don't." Cole shook his head warningly. "I'll do this, but no more plans, please. I'm here to check out operations in the hotel, and if you're not going to let me do that, I'll call Uncle Bill and tell him his sister is being difficult."

"My brother may oversee the hotel chain, but at the Stratton, I'm the boss." Ida pushed him out the door of her suite. "Thanks, honey, I really appreciate this. See you this afternoon."

Paloma Street was located a few blocks from downtown and the Napa River. Small, charming cottages sat on large lots filled with trees, greenery, and other vegetation, giving a somewhat rural vibe to the neighborhood. He couldn't quite imagine one of his aunt's cronies living here, but at least his motorcycle didn't look out of place.

As he paused at a stop sign, two male teenagers working on a beat-up car gave his bike a long look, and he couldn't help but smile to himself. A few years ago, he would not have thought one second about impressing a couple of kids with the roar of a motorcycle. Entrepreneurs and big-business CEOs had been his targets. He'd certainly come a long way from his days of expensive Italian suits, private planes, and high-end cars.

Some of his friends would say he'd gone down—way down. Maybe he had, but it felt a lot better to have the sun on his skin and the wind at his back than to be sitting in an office fifteen hours a day making another buck to spend on something he wouldn't have time to enjoy.

This was the life. No strings, no attachments, no messy personal relationships...and nothing to tie him down. He would not get caught up in the trap of commitment again. Now, the only thing he valued was freedom.

As he continued down the street, he checked the addresses, realizing that the house he was looking for sat at the end of the cul-de-sac, fringed with a thick patch of tall eucalyptus trees. The one-story home was painted bright white with blue shutters adorning the windows. There were tall hedges on both sides of the property. A large utility truck blocked his view of the driveway, and he took the turn a little faster than he should have. Although he'd gotten used to the bike on his long ride up from LA, he still wasn't an expert, and the wheelbarrow in the middle of the driveway took him completely by surprise.

Swearing under his breath, he pulled the bike quickly to the right, and hung on tight as the powerful machine ran off the driveway, through a garden and finally came to rest on the middle of the front lawn. He hoped Aunt Ida's friend had a sense of humor.

The front door opened, followed by a feminine shriek

of alarm and the sound of the screen door banging in disapproval. He winced to himself and slowly removed his helmet, then turned his head, prepared to offer a heartfelt apology.

"Oh my God, you've killed Henry," she said.

He didn't know which surprised him more—her cryptic words, or the fact that the woman his aunt had sent him to meet was the beautiful redhead from the hotel, who had appeared in a few of his dreams the night before.

"I can't believe it," she muttered, her gaze meeting his. "You? What are you doing here?"

"My aunt sent me here, and who's Henry?"

"I hope to God you missed him, because there is no way I could grow another one like him in a week."

Cole followed Maggie across the lawn to a garden not only thick with vines but also covered with sheets. "Who is Henry?" he asked, really hoping there wasn't a body under those sheets.

Maggie knelt on the ground and pulled the sheet away to reveal an incredibly massive pumpkin. "This is Henry and he looks okay, thank goodness." She patted the pumpkin with her hand. "No scars or scratches." She blew out a breath of relief.

Cole squatted down next to her. "Do you always name your vegetables?"

"Only my favorites, and this one is very, very special. He's going to win me a blue ribbon in the Harvest Festival next week. I've entered the pumpkin growing competition. I can't compete with the giant pumpkins, but I think I have a chance in the next division down. Henry looks to weigh about a hundred pounds, and he's pretty, too, so he should get high marks on symmetry and color. I just hope the trauma of having your motorcycle almost run him over won't stunt his growth. He grows about two inches every night."

Cole smiled, thinking the redhead might be pretty but she was apparently also a little crazy. "Maybe you should send old Hank to a pumpkin doctor just to be sure there are no long-lasting effects."

Maggie sent him a disgusted look. "Ha-Ha. You obviously don't appreciate a good pumpkin."

"I prefer my pumpkin in a pie. I'll bet Hank would be tasty. What do you say we just cut him open?"

Cole teasingly reached for the pumpkin, but Maggie grabbed his wrist. "Don't you dare!"

Her abrupt move sent her tumbling against him. He lost his balance and ended up flat on his back in the dirt. There was a hard rock under his spine, but having Maggie on top of him was pretty damn hot. Her full breasts pressed against his chest. Her cheeks were red with anger, her blue eyes parking with indignation, and her beautiful strawberry blonde hair tumbled around her shoulders.

Her mouth called to him as it had the day before, her soft lips beckoning with a sweet sensuality that was both enticing and terrifying, because as much as he liked to have fun with a beautiful woman, he had the feeling that having fun with Maggie would take him places he did not want to go.

It was that self-preservation instinct that made him set Maggie to the side and get to his feet.

He held out his hand and helped Maggie up. "I was just kidding," he said.

She brushed the dirt off the back of her shirt and jeans and gave him an irritated frown. "Tell me again why you're here."

"Aunt Ida told me you were going to take me to

breakfast and show me downtown Napa."

"Aunt Ida?" she echoed with a raise of her brow. "You're Mrs. Stratton's nephew?"

He nodded. He was supposed to be working undercover at the hotel, but since his aunt had already put this meeting in motion, there was no point in denying their relationship.

"I thought you were a teenager. She said she was going to drop you off, that you were a sweet boy."

"I am a sweet boy," he said with a laugh.

"You haven't been a boy in a very long time, and sweet doesn't fit you, either. This is not what I agreed to."

"Hey, I'm as much in the dark as you are. I thought you were going to be a woman of my aunt's generation. Although, this is just like Aunt Ida; she enjoys setting me up with single, attractive women."

"I can't imagine why she'd want to set us up." Maggie's mouth tightened, and a new suspicious gleam appeared in her eyes. "Why did you come into the hotel like any other guest if you're the nephew of the owner? Why did your aunt let us give you the worst room in the hotel?"

"At least you admit it's the worst room."

"You didn't answer either of my questions."

"Aunt Ida told me to check in when I arrived. I'm sure she didn't anticipate me getting the worst room in the hotel."

"If you'd told me who you were, that wouldn't have happened."

"I don't like to drop names," he said, not able to tell her the real reason he hadn't used his aunt's name. "So, are you up for breakfast? Because I'm starving."

She hesitated. "I suppose. I just need to take a pie out

of the oven. Why don't you come in for a minute?"

"Is it all right for us to leave Henry alone?" he teased.

She made a face at him. "I'm sure he'll be fine as soon as I get you out of my garden. Why didn't you just stop in the driveway?"

"I took the turn a little too fast. That truck blocked my vision."

"Sure. That sounds about right," she said dryly. "I bet you do everything a little too fast."

He smiled back at her. "I can go slow—with the right motivation."

Her cheeks warmed and she shook a finger at him. "You need to behave."

"Do I?"

She paused on the step in front of her door. "If you want to come in, you do."

"Fine, I'll be good." *For now*, he silently added.

Chapter Three

⟶ ⇒⇒ ⇇⇇ ⇐

Despite Cole's promise to behave, Maggie felt a little unsettled by his presence in her small house. As they walked down the hall and into her kitchen, she was acutely aware of the fact that he towered over her by at least six inches, and there was a power and athleticism about his body that made her imagine a magnificent body under his jeans and light gray t-shirt.

She'd been right about the tattoo she realized, seeing a phoenix on his right bicep as she turned to ask him if he wanted some coffee.

He caught her staring and raised an eyebrow. "What?"

She cleared her throat. "I just noticed your tattoo. Why did you choose a phoenix?"

"No reason, really," he said vaguely.

Seeing the shadows in his eyes, she didn't believe that for a second.

"So you've been doing some baking, I see." Cole swept his hand toward the mess of flour and dough on her kitchen island.

"I was testing out a new apple pie recipe. I'm going to enter the pie in the Harvest Festival as well as Henry. My mother used to make an incredible pie, but she died before I ever got the recipe, and I've been trying to recreate it. So far, I have not been successful." She opened the oven door and took her latest pie out and set it on the counter.

"It looks good," he said.

It did look pretty on the outside with the apple juice bubbling through the lattice crust, but the inside filling would be the true test. "We'll see. Do you want some coffee?"

"I'd love some. And I wouldn't mind a piece of that pie, either. Think of me as an objective judge."

She hesitated and then figured she might as well get another opinion. "Sure, why not? The plates are in the cupboard." She tipped her head to the cupboard by the sink.

While Cole cut himself a piece of pie, she filled two mugs with coffee and then met him by the island.

His first bite of pie was followed by a wry grimace. He chewed and then swallowed with some relief.

"What do you think?" she asked, seeing the truth in his eyes. "Not good?"

"Uh, it's different," he said carefully.

"You don't have to be polite. I need an honest opinion."

"Everyone wants honesty until they actually get it. Then it's a different story. I don't fall into that trap anymore."

"I can take it," she said. "I really do want to know. I can't enter a bad pie in the competition."

"Fine. The pie is terrible. I never imagined anything that looks this pretty could taste that bad." He picked up the coffee mug and took a long drink. "Now, I've hurt your feelings, haven't I?"

She sighed and grabbed her own fork. She scooped up a bite of pie and then grimaced at the clashing flavors. "You're right. It's terrible. I had a feeling the ingredients were off. I tasted the filling before I put it in the oven, but I thought it might get better with cooking. I'll have to try again." She paused. "If you don't want to go out to breakfast, I could make you some eggs here."

"Can you, Maggie?" he asked doubtfully.

She made a face at him. "The pie is not a true example of my cooking abilities. There's some ingredient that's evading my memory, and I keep trying new things to figure out what I'm missing. But scrambled eggs are a different story."

"I'd still rather go out. My aunt wants me to see downtown. Let's start with a good breakfast café."

"There is a nice place a few blocks away. We can walk."

"Or I can give you a ride."

"Can you, Cole?" she said with a teasing smile, echoing his earlier words. "I've seen your driving skills."

He grinned back at her. "I guess we haven't seen each other at our best yet. Let's walk into town and start over."

She liked the sound of that, especially the part where she got Cole out of her house.

After she grabbed her purse and a sweater, they headed out the door and down the street. It was a cool, sunny morning, and she was happy to put on the sweater over her jeans and knit top.

"Nice neighborhood," Cole commented. "Have you lived here long?"

"Almost a year. I love it. It's quiet, but it's also close to the action—the best of both worlds."

"I'm surprised someone your age is happy with quiet. You don't get bored?"

His question wasn't surprising. Every single one of her friends thought she was crazy to want to buy a house and live so far away from the city, but she knew what she wanted, because she'd wanted it for a very long time. "You can be bored anywhere. It's not about geography. I'm twenty-seven. I've done the big city. I lived in San Francisco for four years after college. It was too crowded and noisy for me. I much prefer this beautiful valley to the crowded, congested, urban streets."

"Where you can bake pies and grow pumpkins."

"And work at the Stratton, which is a lot of fun. I'm very social there. Sometimes, it's nice to get away from people."

"Now that I do understand."

"What about you, Cole? Where do you call home?"

"Los Angeles."

"So you're a Southern California guy. That seems right. You have a nice tan." She could picture him running on the beach, his hair blowing in the wind, his body glistening with sweat. Her heart beat a little too fast, and she took in a calming breath. "What do you do for a living?"

"I—freelance."

"Freelance what?"

"This and that," he said vaguely.

She raised an eyebrow as she cast a thoughtful look at him. "Why are you being so vague? Are you a spy? A criminal? A beach volleyball player?"

He laughed. "Are those my only choices?"

"No, I could go on. Do you want me to keep guessing?"

"That won't be necessary. I'm actually between jobs at the moment. I worked really hard for a long time and a few years ago, I decided to take some time off to travel and see what I'd been missing."

"That sounds fun. What did you do before you were between jobs?" she pressed.

"You're a little nosy."

"And you're a little cagey, which makes me more curious."

He let out a sigh. "I'm not hiding an exciting secret. I was a venture capitalist. I worked for a large corporate firm that bought and sold companies all over the world."

"Really?" His answer surprised her. "I picture a venture capitalist in a dark suit with a silk tie, short hair styled at the best salon in town, a clean-shaven face, and definitely not a tattoo."

"You just described what I used to look like," he admitted.

"What happened?"

"I decided to make a change."

"Why?"

"I didn't like what I was doing, what I was becoming, so I quit."

"That sounds like the short version of a long story."

"The long version is boring."

She doubted that, and she had to admit she was intrigued. Her first impression of Cole Hastings had obviously not been completely accurate. She definitely hadn't pegged him for a venture capitalist. On the other hand, it didn't appear he was doing much of anything anymore, and that did fit with her first impression. "Does the phoenix tattoo represent your rebirth?"

He glanced down at her as they paused at an

intersection. "In a way. I wanted a reminder to live my own life, not someone else's." He gave her a lazy grin. "It hurt like a son of a bitch."

She laughed. "I wouldn't know. I'm not a big fan of needles. The most dangerous I ever got was a belly button ring, but I was eighteen and stupid at the time."

"Do you still have it?"

"No. I realized it was not me." She wondered if the tattoo was really him, but he was moving on.

"Let's talk about you, Maggie. Have you always worked in hotels?"

"Since I was in college," she said as they crossed the street. "I started as an intern and then after graduation, I got a job at a Holiday Inn in San Francisco. I was there two years and then moved on to a Marriott. The chains were okay; I learned a lot, but I really wanted to go more upscale. When I saw a job opening for the Stratton about a year ago, I took it. And I love working there. It's such a grand hotel and yet warm and cozy at the same time. It feels like a home away from home."

"My aunt should hire you to be her company spokesperson," Cole said dryly.

"That would be a fun job. I like working for your aunt. We missed her when she spent several months traveling through Europe and Asia. It's nice to have her back. I feel like she's going to continue to make positive changes at the hotel."

"What kind of changes would those be?"

She hesitated, not wanting to complain about the Stratton to a guest who was also the owner's nephew. "Oh, I don't know. Just small things here and there. I'm sure your aunt is aware of the problem areas."

"Would one of those problems be the uptight man

who forced you to give me a bad room?"

"Mr. Stone is the manager of the hotel, and he can be a little rigid," she said carefully. "But you did deliberately cause a scene in the lobby, so you can't really blame him for paying you back the way he did."

"I wouldn't call kissing you making a scene. There were four people in the lobby, hardly a crowd."

"That didn't matter. Mr. Stone has very specific ideas about behavior in the hotel, especially from his employees. You put me in an awkward situation."

"Sorry about that. I really didn't think it was a big deal."

"Even though you were totally making up an imaginary woman named Kathy?" she challenged.

He laughed and flung her an unrepentant look. "The kiss was worth it."

Her lips tingled at the memory of that crazy kiss. "Maybe to you, but I got another black mark on my work record."

"I can explain to your boss that it was completely my fault."

She sighed. "No. I appreciate the offer, but it wouldn't make a difference. Mr. Stone is not a big fan of mine. He hovers behind me just waiting for me to screw up."

"Why would he do that?"

"I'm not really sure; I obviously did something to piss him off. But I'm doing my best to stay on his good side. I love working at the Stratton, and I need my job, so I try to do what I'm told."

They walked across the bridge, the Napa River flowing beneath, and she paused so he could take a better look.

"The river is low," he commented.

"We haven't had a good rain in a while. When the storms do come, the river sometimes overflows and spills into the downtown streets. We had some heavy flooding a couple of years ago about a mile from here. Some of the buildings were damaged beyond repair. The good news is that they're now developing the area into a beautiful open-air shopping mall that's going to be good for tourists and good for the Stratton."

"Is it open yet?"

"A few of the restaurants have begun service, but most of the mall will be open next year. Have you been to Napa before?"

"Not for at least ten years. I'm sure a lot has changed."

"Probably. But despite the progress of recent years, the town works hard to keep its charm."

They walked over the bridge, and she took him down a side street to the Hummingbird Café, her favorite place for breakfast. The restaurant was busy, as was usual on the weekends, but they were lucky enough to get a corner booth within a few moments.

"The blueberry waffles are the house specialty," Maggie told Cole as they sat down. Her stomach grumbled as she opened the menu. She'd been so consumed with getting a pie baked before Ida's mysterious nephew appeared that she hadn't had anything to eat except that one awful bite of her failed pie.

"I'm putting waffles at the top of the list," Cole said, putting down the menu. When the waitress came, he added in scrambled eggs, hash browns, and bacon to his list.

Maggie ordered a vegetable omelet and fruit as well

as a cup of coffee. Then she said, "So why aren't you having breakfast with your aunt?"

"Apparently, there's some convention at the hotel, and she didn't think I'd fit in."

"That's true, but I doubt you care much about fitting in."

He smiled as he sipped his coffee. Now that he'd removed his sunglasses, she was struck by how dark and intense his eyes were. As her gaze ran down the rest of his face, taking in the scruffy beard, the strong jaw, and the firm, demanding mouth that had been on hers not too long ago, she cleared her throat and reached for her water glass. She needed something to cool her down.

"I used to care about fitting in. I don't anymore. It's quite freeing not to give a damn about what other people think. You might want to try it."

"I don't care all that much about what people think," she said defensively.

He raised an eyebrow. "Are you sure about that? I saw the way you rolled over for your boss."

"I didn't stand up to my boss because I need my job, not because I'm afraid to speak up. I'm trying to buy a house, and I need three more paychecks to make the down payment. Until then, whatever Mr. Stone wants me to do, I do."

Cole gave her a thoughtful and somewhat surprised look. "You're going to buy a house?"

"Yes. I have a lease with an option to buy, but my landlord can only give me two more months to come up with the cash before he puts the house on the market. It's really expensive here, so this kind of deal is my best shot at owning a home."

"But why buy a house now? You're young and single.

Why tie yourself down and become a slave to a mortgage payment?"

"Because I want a home." She could see the doubt in his eyes and wanted to explain. "I'm an Army brat, Cole. I spent my childhood following my father around the world. I went to three elementary schools, two middle schools and two high schools. I hated always being the new kid, the one who didn't have friends from kindergarten on, the one who didn't quite fit in. And when I would make friends, we would have to move again. I hated being constantly uprooted."

"That makes sense," Cole said with a nod. "I guess I can see why you'd want roots, but you're still young. What if you meet someone and they don't want to live in Napa?"

"Then they probably wouldn't be the right person for me."

"You'd choose your house over a person who loved you?" he challenged.

There was a glint of anger in his eyes now, and she sensed that he wasn't talking about her anymore. "I don't know that it has to come to that," she said carefully. "And it's not like I have someone in my life right now to factor in to the decision. I have to take care of myself, make my own home."

"Where's your family now?"

"My father is in Germany. He's a two-star general in the Army. My two brothers are also in the Army; they followed in my dad's footsteps. One is deployed to the Middle East and the other is in North Carolina. We're all spread out."

"And your mom?"

His words sent a stabbing pain through her body.

"She died when I was seventeen. It was a freak accident. She was at the grocery store shopping for dinner, and someone driving into the parking lot had a heart attack and drove through the store windows. Two people were injured and my mom was killed instantly."

Shock filled Cole's eyes. He reached across the table and put his hand over hers where it rested on the table. "I'm sorry, Maggie. That's awful."

Her throat tightened. "It was really bad. My world shattered into a thousand pieces."

He shook his head. "I'm sorry I asked."

"Don't be. I miss her, but I like to think about her and to talk about her." She paused. "My mom was my only anchor in a life of constant changes. No matter where we went, she was there. No matter how hard the days at a new school were, I knew she would be waiting with a smile when I got home. I was the youngest, so after the boys enlisted, it was just my mom and me in the house. We had a good time together," she said with a sad smile. "She was loving, kind, and funny. I could tell her anything. She wouldn't judge; she'd just listen."

"She sounds great," Cole said.

"She was amazing. I was so angry after she died. It seemed unfair and wrong to me. Not that I wanted anything to happen to my father, but my dad was the one I was supposed to worry about and then my brothers. They were the ones in danger. But she was the one to die." She drew in a breath. "My dad got leave to come home while I finished my last month of high school. But as soon as I went off to college, he returned to his career. It felt strange, like we never really mourned my mom as a family unit for more than a few weeks. I guess everyone did it in their own way, but aside from the funeral, we weren't able to spend any time together just talking about her." She paused, giving him an apologetic smile. "I don't know why I'm telling you all this."

"Because I asked," he said simply.

"I'll bet you're sorry you did that."

"Not at all. College must have been difficult. You were away from home, still grieving…"

"I was a mess. But I made some really good girlfriends freshman year, and I know that they're the reason I made it through those first two years. Holidays were hard, of course, but there was no home to go back to. My dad sold the house we were living in when my mom died, so I'd travel to wherever he was for Christmas or Thanksgiving. Sometimes, I just went home with friends." She licked her lips. "Which brings me around to why I really want my own house. I want a place where my family can gather and celebrate the holidays the way we used to when my mom was alive. I feel like I owe it to her to try to bring everyone back together. I think she would hate that we're so spread apart and disconnected."

"I understand. I hope you get what you want, and I hope…" His voice drifted away.

"What?" she asked curiously.

He shrugged. "It doesn't matter."

"You were going to say something—just say it."

He met her gaze. "Sometimes what you think you want, what you think you should have, is not what you really need."

She stared back at him, her brows drawing together. "Are we talking about me or you?"

He tipped his head. "You're quick. I need to remember that."

"And you've dodged the question, Cole."

"Maybe I was talking more about me," he conceded. "From the day I graduated college until two years ago I went head down, pedal to the metal, chasing what I thought I wanted. It turned out it was a huge mistake."

"Why?" she asked curiously.

"Because in the end, none of it mattered."

"Are you at the *end*, Cole? You're not that much older than me. Thirty-one, thirty-four?"

"Thirty-two."

"You have a lot of life ahead of you before you get to the end. Maybe it's too soon to make judgments."

"I could say the same for you, Maggie. You act like buying your house is the end of your lifelong dream. Is there going to be another dream for you?"

"I'll figure that out after I get this one. What about you? What's your dream now?"

"I'm living my dream. I do what I want, go where I want, and I have absolute and total freedom. I have no one to account to except myself."

"Well, I hope that in the *end*," she said pointedly, "you'll be happy that you chose freedom over everything else."

He smiled. "I hope so, too. But right now I think we should stop worrying about the future and enjoy our breakfast." He sat back as the waiter set down their eggs and waffles.

Her stomach grumbled with delight. "That sounds like a good plan."

Chapter Four

Over breakfast, Maggie steered the conversation away from personal topics. She couldn't quite believe she'd told Cole so much about her mom and her childhood. She couldn't remember the last time she'd discussed her mother with anyone, much less a man she'd met the day before.

She had to admit Cole was a good listener, which was probably why she'd rambled on. It had been a nice change of pace to be with a man who seemed genuinely interested in what she had to say, but she was a little embarrassed by how much she'd shared. Thankfully, Cole was happy to go along with new topics and after they left the café she showed him around the downtown area, pointing out the historic buildings and the new businesses that were bringing more tourists into town. While Napa was known for its valley of wineries, the city offered a multitude of art galleries, and restaurants offering everything from organic vegan to fine dining with celebrity chefs. The city also had a plethora of clothing boutiques, both vintage and upscale, jewelry stores featuring local artists, and one of the best homemade ice-cream parlors in the county.

She finished their tour at a small park along the river.

The sun had risen higher in the sky and was warming up the crisp air. She pulled off her sweater and tied it around her waist as she and Cole sat down on a bench overlooking the water.

"This is nice," he commented.

"It's one of my favorite spots," she agreed. "The river feels calming. I take a lot of walks along the water."

"I usually prefer to jog than to walk."

"You're a runner?"

"Three to four times a week," he said. "What about you?"

"No," she said with a shake of her head. "Running is not my thing. I will get on the elliptical at the gym but only if I have music in my ears or a TV to watch."

He smiled. "And I thought you were a woman who liked nature."

"For a walk or a drive or even a bike ride, but not a run. That's way too much work, and I spend so much time thinking about how far I have to go before I can stop that I don't enjoy it at all."

"Running can be mental as well as physical. For me, there's nothing better than running toward something new and exciting."

"I'm beginning to sense a trend with you, Cole. You quit your job. You travel. You like to run. Are you really running toward something? Or are you running away from something?"

He turned his head to look at her, a somber glint in his dark eyes. "Maybe both."

She was intrigued by his answer and wanted to hear more, but he didn't seem inclined to expand on the subject. Instead, he said, "Tell me about the wineries."

"Well, what do you want to know?" she countered.

"There are about four hundred wineries in Napa."

He raised an eyebrow. "Seriously?"

"Wine is Napa's very serious business. You should go to some of the more interesting wineries while you're here. Your aunt buys wine for the hotel from several of the local vineyards."

"I was planning on doing some wine tasting tomorrow."

"I'd start early and make a day of it. I can give you some recommendations on good wineries to visit, not just for the wine, but also for the atmosphere, the cool wine cellars, and beautiful hillside vineyards."

"So you've been to a lot of wineries?"

"Not all four hundred," she said with a laugh. "But I've been to least a dozen."

"It sounds like you would make the perfect guide."

"I'm sure your aunt would like to spend time with you, and she would definitely be the perfect guide."

"Unfortunately, she seems to be tied up this weekend. She told me earlier that I probably wouldn't see much of her until next week."

She nodded. "I know that several of her friends are involved with the convention going on this weekend. I'm surprised she didn't tell you about it so you could coordinate your travel."

"My fault more than hers. I wasn't clear on what date I'd be arriving until about three days ago." He uncrossed his arms, putting one along the back of the bench behind her head as he shifted to face her. "I have an idea."

Judging by the mischievous gleam in his gaze, she didn't think it was going to be a good one. "What's that?"

"You could give me a tour of the wineries tomorrow—unless you're working?"

"I'm actually off tomorrow," she admitted.

"Then you're free."

"I didn't say I was free. I do have a life. I have things to do. I usually run errands on my day off."

"Errands don't sound as fun as wine tasting. And just think, you'd be doing my aunt a big favor."

"I already did her a favor by having breakfast with you."

He smiled. "True, but you'd earn even more points by showing me around the valley."

Remembering her conversation with Ida Stratton, she had a feeling he was right. Mrs. Stratton had asked her to help entertain her nephew. If Cole hadn't been a sexy bad boy who could kiss like the devil, would she be hesitating at all? Probably not.

"All right," she said, pushing away the last of her doubts. It might be a bad idea to spend more time with Cole. On the other hand, she could use Mrs. Stratton on her side in case her boss went even more psycho in his micromanagement. "I'll go with you."

"Great."

"It's too bad you weren't here last month for the annual crush of the grapes. Maybe next year."

"Maybe. Who knows where I'll be next September? I could be anywhere."

His freedom-loving lifestyle had some appeal, but it wasn't for her. She didn't need to travel; she'd already lived in far too many places. Freedom for her meant being able to stay in one place.

"We have one thing in common," she said.

He shot her a curious look. "We do? What's that?"

"We're both going after our dreams, putting ourselves first."

"That's true." He gave her a speculative look. "Tell me something—why don't you have a man in your life?"

She smiled. "Let's see. I name my ridiculously large pumpkins, I make poisonous apple pies, and I want to live in a little house for the rest of my life. I'm boring as hell. Most nights I'm in bed by ten. You think men are lining up for that?"

He grinned. "I don't think you're boring, Maggie. You're—unique."

"Unique, huh? I guess I've heard worse."

"In a good way. And you're a beautiful woman. I don't think you'll scare anyone away with Henry or a bad pie."

She self-consciously tucked a strand of hair behind her ear as his gaze rested on her face, the expression in his eyes way too full of male appreciation, the kind of regard that made goose bumps run down her arms. "I'm not interested in a relationship right now," she said, trying to ignore the butterflies in her stomach. "I have other goals that are more pressing."

"Like your house."

"Like my house," she agreed. "I've seen a lot of my friends fall in love over the past year, and while it's awesome and I'd love to find that kind of connection with someone, in reality I'm still trying to find myself."

He nodded thoughtfully. "That's smart, Maggie. Most people don't think that way; I know I didn't."

"You didn't?"

He frowned, as if he suddenly realized he'd slipped up.

"Okay, who was she?" Maggie asked. "What was her name? And don't try to tell me there's no one, because I don't think you changed your whole life around without a woman being somewhere in the mix."

He stared back at her. "You're right. There was a woman. Her name was—is—Carole. We met in grad school at UCLA. I was getting an MBA in business, and so was she. We had so much in common back then. It seemed like we were on exactly the same page. I was a year ahead of Carole and after I got my degree, I asked her to marry me. She said yes and the next thing I knew she was dropping out of school to plan the wedding, and I was hired by her father to work in his investment firm."

She was surprised by just about everything he'd said. "You have a master's degree in business administration?"

He nodded. "Yep."

"And you got married when you were…"

"Twenty-six. Old enough to know better. Young enough to still be a little stupid."

"So what happened?"

"The wedding took a year to plan. During that time I worked a million hours. We thought once we got married and got settled, we'd spend more time together. But then there was a house to buy. Carole wanted to live in the same neighborhood as her parents, and they were rich. They wanted to help us, but my pride wouldn't allow them to pay for everything, so I said I'd find a way to pay for half, which meant I worked more hours. We got the house, and Carole instantly decided to remodel and redecorate, which took another year of our lives." He paused. "Three years into the marriage we finally had time to look at each other, and we didn't even recognize ourselves. But we did know one thing—we weren't happy."

"So you got a divorce?"

"Yes, our marriage came to an official end a few days

before what would have been our fourth wedding anniversary. I quit my job the same day. It was a hell of a day."

She gave him a compassionate smile, seeing the pain in his eyes. "I can't even imagine."

"The end was actually easier than all the rest of it, because I was done, because I realized I'd been living someone else's life, someone else's dream. I'd lost myself in a relationship and a marriage that wasn't right for either party. I'm glad Carole found someone she could be happy with."

"Maybe you will, too."

"Possibly, but I'm not in a hurry. I like my life where it is now. I'm free."

"You've always been free to make your own choices. You just made bad choices," she couldn't help pointing out.

He tipped his head to her point. "That's true. I realized that on a road somewhere in South America about four months ago. I can't regret the choices I made, and I can't look back. So I look forward and I try to make better decisions."

She nodded. "I now understand why you've been so scornful of my desire to own a house. I must remind you of your wife."

"Actually, you are nothing like Carole," he said with a smile. "Except for your desire to own a home. But she didn't want just a house; she wanted a mansion. She wanted the country-club lifestyle of her parents, and I never wanted that."

"Neither do I. I'd be super happy with my charming, rustic, two-bedroom house with the big garden."

"It's still a house, Maggie. It can still weigh you

down."

"I'd relish that weight."

"You say that now, and you may think having a house will be the answer to all your problems and the realization of all your dreams, but in reality it's just a building. It's not going to change your childhood."

"It doesn't have to change the past—just the future."

"Well, I hope you get what you want."

"I will. I'm determined."

"I can see that," he said with a warm smile.

"So would you ever get married again, Cole?"

"I don't know. I don't think about it."

"Don't you want to have kids someday?"

"Kids need roots, as you've so recently reminded me; I travel light these days."

"You might get tired of that."

"I doubt it."

She wondered about that. "My grandmother used to say that you can lock up the barn after the horse runs away, but your horse is still gone."

He laughed. "Okay. I think I get what you mean, but I prefer to think of myself as being the runaway horse and not the person locking the barn door a little too late."

"I'm just saying maybe you're overreacting a little, throwing out everything instead of just cutting out the problem parts of your life. You were in grad school before you met Carole. You must have had your own business dreams."

"I did, but the reality of those dreams didn't turn out to be what I wanted. And you should ask yourself the same question. Are you overreacting to your past, trying to force a future that you're not ready for? Why not wait until you get married and have kids before tying yourself to a mortgage?"

"Because I have an opportunity now, and sometimes when a door opens, you have to go in, because it may not open again."

"Well, I know better than anyone that I can't talk people out of what they want to do, so I wish you luck, Maggie."

"Thank you. I wish you luck, too. But I do have a question."

"Another one?"

"Yes. You're Ida Stratton's nephew, and I know a little about the Stratton family. Ida's parents started a hotel chain sixty years ago and Ida and her six siblings now overseen a dozen hotels around the world. You didn't grow up poor. I'm guessing that you come from money, too. Was it really just Carole who wanted the country-club life?"

"I did not grow up with money. My mother was the black sheep of the Stratton family. There were seven siblings in my mother's generation, five brothers and two sisters. My mom was the youngest and the most rebellious. She had a falling out with my grandfather when she married my dad—a man my grandfather did not approve of."

"Why not? Was he a bad boy biker, too?" she teased.

He grinned. "He didn't like motorcycles, but he played guitar in a band and picked up odd jobs on the side to fuel his love of music. He wasn't ambitious or driven, and he came from absolutely no money. My grandfather thought he was a gold digger and told my mom he would cut her off if she married my father. My mother doesn't respond well to ultimatums. She said she didn't care about the Stratton money or the family business. She married my dad, moved across the country from her family, and I grew up without any relatives for a very long time. Eventually, when I was probably around ten or so, some of my mother's siblings, including Ida, came around, and they made up, but my mother was still out of the business."

"Where do your parents live now?"

"Los Angeles. My dad teaches music. My mother sells real estate. They're happy as can be. I will admit that I did want to make a better life for myself than the one I grew up in which is why I went to business school. But apparently there's more of my rebellious mother and dreamer father in me than I realized."

"You didn't have any siblings?"

"No. My mom said I was the miracle child. Apparently she had trouble getting pregnant."

"So you grew up the adored only miracle child," she said dryly. "That explains a lot."

He smiled. "You think I'm entitled?"

"Yes. I think you're used to being the center of attention. That's why you kissed me yesterday. You knew the impression you were making in the hotel, and you wanted to make the light on you just a little brighter."

His grin broadened as a sparkle ran through his eyes. "Maybe I was just really attracted to you."

"I don't think so," she said, wishing now that she hadn't brought that kiss up again.

"Are you sure about that? Because I can feel the electricity between us right now. And I'm betting you can, too, Maggie." His hand drifted from the back of the bench to her shoulder, and she felt a wave of heat run through her. That heat got a little hotter as his fingers teased the curve of her neck, as he slid down the bench so his thigh was against hers.

She didn't want to admit the attraction, but judging by the knowing gleam in his eyes, he'd know she was lying.

"Even if there is a little chemistry between us," she said, "I wouldn't act on it."

"Why not? You're single. I'm single." He dropped his voice down a notch as he leaned in. "We could have some fun together."

He was so close she could feel his breath on her face. They could definitely have some fun together, but then what? She drew in a breath and let it out, trying to rein in the desire that had so quickly escalated. "We might have fun today, but tomorrow or the next day or the next week would not be fun at all. I don't do bad boys anymore."

"Anymore?" he queried with an arch of his eyebrow.

She hesitated. "I ran a little wild in college. After my mom died, I was pissed off, not just because of her death, but because my father had pushed me to go away to school when I didn't feel ready. But he was ready to go back to work, so I had to be ready, too."

"So you were angry with him."

"With the world. I spent the first two years of college partying with long-haired, tattooed boys with sexy smiles and hot bodies and not much else going on."

"Now you've surprised me," Cole said.

"I'm not proud of who I was then. Thankfully, I had good girlfriends who stopped me from doing anything too stupid. Eventually, I came to my senses and started focusing on school and not ruining the rest of my life. Now I date men who at least have the potential of sticking around for a while."

"Not every date has to lead to something more. Not every kiss has to mean something."

"I know that. I just told you that I didn't let anything have meaning for a long time."

"Look who just threw out the baby with the bathwater," he said, echoing her earlier words. "Sometimes a kiss is just a kiss—a moment in time. A really good moment." His mouth covered hers, and this kiss was nothing like the lighthearted caress of the day before. This was a full-on sensuous, demanding kiss, and she opened her mouth to his, welcoming his tongue inside her mouth as his arms tightened around her body.

He tasted like maple syrup, and the sugar on his lips mixed with the hardness of his chest against hers was impossible to resist. Her breasts tingled, her blood pounded through her veins, and everything else in the world faded away. It was just Cole and his mouth, his touch, his desire—and hers.

Cole finally ended the kiss.

She sat back, breathless and a little dizzy.

Cole looked shell-shocked.

"What the hell was that?" he murmured.

"It was nothing. Like you said, sometimes a kiss is just a kiss." She jumped to her feet, adrenaline making her want to move and walking away would be better than grabbing Cole and throwing herself back into his arms. "We should walk back. I have some errands to run before I go to work later."

Cole caught up to her with a few long strides. She was both happy and a little unsettled that he didn't speak to her on their way back to the house, but since she had no idea what to say to him, she needed to be grateful for the silence.

"I'll say good-bye here," she said, pausing next to his bike still parked in the middle of her yard. "Thanks for breakfast."

"Maggie, wait."

"I don't want to talk about it," she said abruptly.

"I feel like I should apologize."

"Please don't. We both know you're not sorry. And neither am I."

"No?" he asked doubtfully.

"No. It was an amazing kiss, but it's not going to happen again. You're just passing through town, and I have a plan to execute. I can't be distracted. So let's say good-bye."

"Not good-bye. You already promised you would go wine tasting with me tomorrow."

Damn! She'd forgotten about that. "I'm going to back out."

"No, you're not."

"It's not a good idea."

"Look, I can promise you that I will not kiss you again. Okay?"

She blew out a breath. Maybe he could promise that, but she wasn't so sure she could make the same promise, because it wasn't just him she was fighting; it was herself.

"Please, Maggie?" he asked, with a persuasive smile. "My aunt is busy, and it's no fun tasting wine alone."

She shook her head, knowing she'd backed herself into a corner. "I would be crazy to say yes."

"Well, we both know you're a little crazy," he said with a laugh. "You do talk to your vegetables."

"Only to Henry," she said, his words bringing a reluctant smile to her lips. "Fine, I'll go with you. We'll taste some wine, but that's it."

"Good. I'll come by here in the morning. If I don't see you at the hotel later today, I'll see you then." He swung his leg over his bike, started the engine and sped out of her yard and down the street.

She had to admit it was a pretty hot exit for a sexy bad boy. Cole was definitely a problem she didn't need. Still, she would probably score points with Ida by taking him wine tasting tomorrow. She could handle one more day in his company. What could go wrong?

Chapter Five

"You're a very bad woman," Cole told his aunt as they ate dinner together in her hotel apartment Saturday night. It was the first opportunity he'd had to speak to her since he'd left Maggie's house earlier in the day.

Ida gave him an unrepentant smile. "What sin have I committed this time?"

"You know perfectly well that you led me to believe Maggie was one of your friends."

"She is a friend."

"And an employee—a young, attractive, single employee."

"She is a beautiful girl with her sparkling blue eyes and that gorgeous blonde hair with the fiery red highlights. I always feel like smiling when I'm with her. I thought you could use a smile, too."

"I'm supposed to be here undercover. Maggie now knows I'm your nephew."

"Did you tell her that you're looking into problems at the hotel?"

"No. Right now she just thinks I'm your nephew, but if I start snooping around, she may get suspicious."

"Oh, I'm sure you'll know how to handle that, and

Maggie is really the least of my worries."

He saw the worry in her eyes. "What are you concerned about? I get the feeling you wanted me to come here for more than just the basic hotel service checkup." Since he'd quit his job, his family had convinced him to freelance consult on their chain of hotel properties. Since that coincided well with his plan to travel and see the world, he'd agreed. A few weeks of work here and there helped fund his travel bank.

"You're right," Ida said. "I recently discovered some anomalies in the books. I asked the accountant, and he very nervously said he must have made a mistake. He then gave me a corrected statement. But there have been other oddities that make me think someone might be stealing from the hotel."

"Like what?"

"I saw an order for a more expensive brand of sheets than we normally use. I asked Harry about it, and he said that was a mistake, that they'd canceled that order and gone back to the original brand."

"So, lots of mistakes," he said slowly.

"All explainable," she said, meeting his gaze. "But my gut tells me there's something going on. I would hate to think that any of my employees are dishonest, but I wasn't here for several months, and it's possible that someone started taking advantage of my inattention. I want you to check things out for me, Cole. I know I can trust you, and you're smart as a whip."

"I'll need access to the books."

"Of course."

"And I'd like to look around the offices."

"Monday would be the best opportunity for that. Mr. Stone is off that day."

"Do you think your manager is involved?"

"I really hope not. He's worked for me for almost six years. On the other hand, he runs the entire operation here, and he was completely in charge while I was traveling. It's difficult to believe anyone could get anything past him. So if something is happening, I have to assume he could be involved." She paused. "Maybe all the mistakes are explainable, and I'm just being paranoid."

"I doubt that. You've always had good instincts."

"I need to get this hotel back on track. Besides the anomalies, our bookings are down, and I don't know why. With the holidays coming, we're usually fully booked months in advance, but now we're at sixty percent occupancy through Christmas. I hate to think we're losing our position as the premiere hotel destination in the Napa Valley, but it's possible."

"We'll figure it out."

"I like your confidence, Cole. I know you'll get to the bottom of things. And I'm hoping you can give me some advice on how to grow the business. My brother Bill didn't want me to take so much time off this past year. He wanted to put in his own manager while I was gone, and I refused. I don't like him looking over my shoulder, and I think of the Stratton as mine. But the family does own a percentage and I really don't want to prove him right. He has such an ego."

Cole laughed. His uncle Bill was definitely arrogant. "I got it. I'll do everything I can to help you, but honestly Aunt Ida if you suspect there's something going on with your staff, you shouldn't have set me up with Maggie. She could be part of whatever is going on here. Hell, she could be the thief."

Ida dismissed that idea with a wave of her hand.

"Don't be silly. You only have to know Maggie for a short while to realize she is completely honest—too honest, probably. The only flaw she seems to have is a soft spot that tends to make her a little less than efficient at times. She gets caught up in conversations, and sometimes the check-in lines get too long."

"Is that what Stone says about her?"

"Among other things. She's not his favorite employee, which I don't really understand, because she's very popular with the guests."

"She was certainly nicer to me when I checked in than your manager was."

"Well, that's because you kissed Maggie and caused a scene."

"Even so, he handled the situation poorly. One of the reasons I come in undercover is to see how all guests are treated, not just the ones wearing suits and carrying high-limit credit cards. Mr. Stone failed the first test."

"I should have him move your room."

He shook his head. "It's fine. And I don't want anyone else to know I'm your nephew, although it's possible Maggie may tell someone. I should talk to her about that tomorrow."

"Tomorrow?" Ida quizzed, a curious gleam appearing in her eyes. "You're seeing Maggie tomorrow?"

"We're going wine tasting," he admitted.

"Well, isn't that interesting?"

"I want to see the wineries since they attract tourists to the hotel, and Maggie knows which ones are the best. Plus, you said you were busy all weekend."

"Sure, of course."

He shook his head at her. "Seriously, you have to stop trying to matchmake, Aunt Ida. I'm not interested in a relationship. And even if I were, Maggie would be the last person in the world I would choose."

"But why? She's beautiful and smart. You could do a lot worse."

"I have done worse."

"Carole and you were too young to get married. You grew up and grew apart. You would make a different choice now."

"If I wanted to make a choice, but I don't. I like being single. I like being free to go where I want. Maggie is a small-town girl with small-town dreams. She's growing pumpkins and baking pies and putting away money to buy a house."

"None of those are bad things," Ida pointed out.

"Not at all, if that's what she wants. But it's not what I want."

Ida sighed. "I'm not sure you know what you want, but suit yourself. I'm not going to do another thing to interfere. I wanted you two to meet. The rest is up to you. I just want you to be happy, Cole."

"I am happy." He set down his napkin and pushed back his chair. "I'll see you tomorrow night."

"Perfect. Have fun tomorrow, Cole."

"I will," he said, trying to ignore the amusement in her eyes. He doubted there was anything he could say that would convince her there was nothing between him and Maggie—maybe   because   there   was something…something hot and heady and irresistible. But he could resist, couldn't he?

Maggie waited for Cole in front of her house just

after eleven on Sunday morning. She had to admit to feeling a bit more excited and anxious than she wanted to feel. She hadn't seen Cole at the hotel the night before, and it bothered her to even secretly admit that she'd spent a lot of time scanning the lobby for any sign of him, but he hadn't come near the front desk.

She'd told herself that was a good thing. Cole was a troublemaker, and Mr. Stone was definitely not a fan of his. The last thing she needed was to get caught up in any battle between the two of them.

She shifted her weight as she pulled out her phone to check for texts. Cole wasn't exactly late, but she was eager to get on with the day.

A moment later, he turned in to her driveway and stopped his bike in the driveway, a good distance away from her pumpkins.

Cole took off his helmet as he got off the bike, giving her a smile as he ran his hand through his dark hair. Damn, he looked good in his worn jeans and light blue button-down shirt with the sleeves rolled up to the elbows. And his aviator sunglasses gave him an even sexier look.

"Thanks for moving the wheelbarrow," he said, as he moved toward her.

"I couldn't risk Henry's life again."

He grinned. "Nor could I. Are you ready to go?"

"Yes. I've picked out five wineries we should check out," she said, handing him a list. "I think we should start at the farthest one first, which is the DeLucca Winery."

"Sounds good to me."

"Why don't I drive us in my car?" she suggested as he put the list in his pocket.

"No way. We'll take my bike. It's a beautiful day."

She frowned. "I'm not big on motorcycles, and I've seen the way you drive."

"I promise I will not let anything happen to you, Maggie."

"Easy to make that promise—harder to keep it. I don't like the idea of there being nothing between me and the ground."

"We'll take back roads. Give it a chance. I think you'll love it. There's nothing like the feeling of the wind against your face and the sun on your back. It's incredible. You won't regret it."

He could definitely be persuasive when he wanted to be. "You won't speed?"

"I promise I won't. Let's get you a helmet."

They walked over to the bike and he took out a helmet for her to put on. Once she'd done that, he said, "Now, get on the bike, wrap your arms around my waist, and we'll ride like the wind."

His enticing words made her suck in a quick breath. She had a feeling Cole was more dangerous than the bike.

In recent years, she had played it safe, but Cole was now reminding her of the more rebellious and adventurous girl she'd once been. She didn't think that was a good thing. But she'd agreed to go wine tasting, and she had on a helmet, so there was only one thing left to do.

Before she could change her mind, she hitched up her short floral skirt and swung her leg over the seat. She wished now she'd worn jeans for this adventure, but she'd dressed more for wine tasting than riding a motorcycle.

Cole turned his head as she got comfortable and placed one hand on her bare thigh. "Slide in a little closer, honey. When we ride this bike, we ride as one."

Maggie swallowed hard and moved closer until her thighs met his. The rough edge of his jeans ground against her bare skin, creating all sorts of unwelcome erotic thoughts in her mind. This was crazy. *What on earth was she thinking?*

"Do you need directions?" she asked, trying to focus her mind on more practical matters.

"I'll put the first address in my phone," he said, taking a minute to do just that. "But I have a good idea where it is. I looked at a map of wineries last night."

"So you would be prepared?" she asked, a little impressed that he'd thought ahead.

He laughed. "Actually, there wasn't much else to do in my room last night, and I was trying to stay away from the sexy redhead at the front desk."

She wasn't going to touch that comment. "Well, at least you know where we're going."

"I do. Hang on," Cole added, pulling her hands in front of his stomach, so tightly she could feel the clench of his abdominal muscles through his shirt. "Let yourself go with the bike. Feel the power. You're going to love this. You'll never be the same. Once you get a taste, you're going to want more."

That was exactly what she was afraid of.

As the powerful engine roared to life, Maggie tightened her arms around Cole. He started out slow, for which she was grateful, increasing his speed once they left her neighborhood.

When they got to the back roads, and the traffic thinned out, she began to relax and actually enjoy the ride. Cole was right. She did like the sun on her face, the wind at her back, and the gorgeous man in front of her.

Cole felt good, too good. She told herself not to get

caught up in her attraction to him. He was not for her. She wanted roots, a place to call home and eventually marriage, kids, maybe a dog. Cole Hastings didn't fit the picture of her future, so there was no point in getting involved with him.

And after yesterday's spectacular kiss, she had to stay on her guard, because if she didn't keep her walls up, she might like him way too much, and that would only lead to heartbreak.

But today was just about wine tasting, something she'd done a dozen times with friends. It would be a fun outing, and that would be it.

Forcing the niggling worries out of her head, she concentrated on the view, the open road, the rolling hills, and vineyards, farms and fruit stands along the highway.

It was a beautiful day. The sky had only occasional wisps of clouds to mar its royal blue hue, and Maggie felt a sense of belonging. This was her land, her home now, and she had picked a good part of the country to set down roots. Everything she wanted was right here.

—➤➤◄◄—

Twenty minutes later, Cole took the turnoff for the DeLucca Winery.

The winery had originally been a cattle ranch, but twenty years ago the DeLucca family had bought the property and turned the barn into a wine cellar and the outer buildings into wine tasting rooms. The Italian family still made their home in the large three-story house at the far end of the property.

Cole pulled into the parking lot, cut the engine and pulled off his helmet. He started to get off, but Maggie's arms were still wrapped around his waist, a sensation she had gotten very used to.

"You can let go of me now," he said, slanting a look in her direction.

She started at his words and then slowly peeled her fingers off his shirt. "Sorry."

"No problem. It might be easier if you got off first, although I won't have as nice a view."

"Right." Maggie tried to hold down her skirt as she swung one leg around the back of the bike and eased herself to the ground. She took off her helmet and shook out her hair.

The look Cole gave her was as potent as a glass of wine, and she felt a delicious tingle run down her spine. If she wasn't careful, she was going to get drunk on Cole today.

"What did you think of the ride?" Cole asked, as he stashed their helmets.

"It wasn't bad," she said, deliberately understating the surprising sense of freedom she'd felt.

He grinned at her. "Well, don't knock yourself out with compliments."

She smiled. "Fine. It was actually more fun than I expected."

"I knew you'd like it. There's still a little rebel inside of you, Maggie."

"I wouldn't go that far. Are you ready to drink some wine?"

"Absolutely," he said, as they made their way to the wine tasting room.

For the next half hour, they toured the winery, learned about its history and the variety of grapes planted on the ten acres adjoining the building, and sipped cabernet sauvignon and merlot, which were both excellent.

Then they walked back to the bike and spent the next two hours touring three more wineries. Maggie felt a little buzzed after the fourth wine tasting, so they stopped at a roadside café and got sandwiches to go, eating their food at a picnic table under a thick patch of trees at the back of the store.

"This is good. I needed something to soak up the wine," Maggie said, as she took another bite of her vegetarian wrap.

"Me, too," Cole replied, making quick work of his roast beef sandwich. "I didn't care much for that last selection of wine. Too dry."

"I agree, and the winemaker was far too pretentious."

"A first-class snob for a third-class wine."

"Exactly. My grandmother used to say if you're going to brag, you better be able to back it up."

"What did you brag about?" he asked with a smile.

"Actually, I think Grandma was talking to my brothers, not me. They were both cocky. Jared was a star athlete. He was a quarterback for one of the high school football teams. Keith was a starting pitcher and a big baseball star. He actually got recruited for the pros, but he went into the Army instead."

"That's quite a choice," Cole commented.

"He wanted to follow in my dad's footsteps; they both did."

"Did you ever consider enlisting?"

"God, no," she said with a shake of her head. "I wouldn't last a minute in basic training. I don't like physical exertion, getting dirty or weapons. I can't even imagine being a soldier."

"Or a soldier's wife."

"Or that," she agreed. "My mother was the perfect soldier's wife. She never complained, always supported my dad, and held the family together when he was gone."

"And she made great pies."

"Yes. What about your mother? Did she bake?"

"Not really. My dad was actually the better cook, but both of them were more interested in other passions like music and art. My mother paints when she's not selling real estate or working whatever day job she's picked up that week. I remember many nights growing up when I'd come home from a practice after school just starving and my mom would be on the porch painting the sunset and my dad would be in the garage working on another song. The stove, of course would be cold. But they were always happy to order out when I reminded them to eat." He smiled. "They were great parents. I have no complaints. I admired their passion. But it was probably good they only had one kid. I don't think there was enough room in their lives for more."

She was beginning to realize that Cole's desire for freedom probably hadn't just come from a bad marriage and a demanding job; he'd had to be responsible for a long time. As a child he'd been the one to think about food, the one to remind his parents to order take-out. No wonder he just wanted to be free.

"Did any of their artistic talents rub off on you?" she asked.

Cole laughed. "Not a single one. I was terrible at the guitar, worse at painting, and I wasn't interested in either. I played sports when I was a kid. I liked soccer and track."

"We're back to running," she said with a smile.

"Yes. What about you? No sports in your past?"

"I was pretty good at volleyball, but that was about it. Since we moved around so much, it was hard to get on to teams. My brothers never had problems because they were so good, but I was barely mediocre. I did like to dance though. I took Irish dancing for quite a few years."

He nodded. "I can see that. You look like you have some Irish in you."

"I do—from my grandmother. The red in my hair comes from her. My mom said I inherited my temper from her."

Cole gave her a doubtful look. "You have a hot temper?"

"When I see injustice. I can't stand when things are blatantly unfair or if someone is just being unkind."

"That sounds like the good side of a temper."

"I didn't know temper had a good side."

"Sometimes it just means you feel passionate about something."

As she gazed into his eyes, she felt that passion he was talking about, and it was for him. She frowned, angry with herself for breaking her own rules and letting down her guard again. It was just a shame that the more she got to know Cole the more she liked him. Usually, it went the other direction.

She crinkled up her wrapper and changed the subject. "That wrap was really good. It hit the spot. I was getting a little fuzzy from the wine. Maybe we should skip the next winery and just go home." Then she could return to her normal life and get Cole out of it.

"There's one more winery I want to go to. It's on a hill, and apparently you have to take a gondola ride to get there. It sounds cool. Have you been to it?"

"No, but I've heard about it."
"One more, Maggie?"
"Okay. Then we call it a day."

Chapter Six

---⇒⇛⇚⇐--

He probably should have agreed to go home, Cole thought, as Maggie got on the bike behind him and wrapped her arms around his waist. Having her so close was a sweet torment. There was nothing worse than wanting something he couldn't have and while there was a part of him that liked the idea of trying to change Maggie's mind, there was another part of him that was very cognizant of the fact that he could not only hurt Maggie, he could hurt himself.

Like Maggie, he had his own plans, and she didn't fit into any one of them. Plus, she worked for his aunt, which put her behind another line he shouldn't cross. It was just too damn bad that she was so sweet and sexy. He liked talking to her more than he'd liked talking to anyone in recent years. Which was probably why he'd told her about Carole and his divorce and quitting his job, three subjects that rarely came up when he was out with a woman. But Maggie was different.

He drew in a breath as her hands tightened around him. He increased his speed, needing the wind in his face to distract him from the woman holding him so close. He'd thought there was nothing sexier than riding a motorcycle. Now he knew that there was nothing hotter than riding a motorcycle with Maggie. Feeling a little reckless, he drove even faster, and soon they were arriving at the next winery.

When he got off the bike and put their helmets away, Maggie gave him a happy smile so inviting he wanted to kiss it right off her lips.

"That was a lot faster than you drove before," she said.

"We had an open road. I thought I'd show you a little more fun." Judging by the light in her eyes, she'd liked it.

"It was fun. I was a little terrified, but I guess that was part of the fun."

"I wouldn't let anything happen to you."

She met his gaze and her smile faded. "It's not always easy to keep that promise. Sometimes life happens."

He had a feeling she was talking about her mom. He flung an arm around her shoulders. "Sometimes," he agreed. "But today it's just about the fun."

She looked up at him. "I have a feeling for you every day is about the fun."

"It is now," he agreed with a laugh. "But shouldn't that be true for everyone?"

She shrugged. "I suppose. But I bet if you worked for Mr. Stone for an hour, you would find fun running in the other direction."

"Don't think about him; it's your day off."

"True. Let's go ride the gondola."

They only had to wait a few moments before boarding the large glass-enclosed gondola. While the gondola was meant to seat four people with two bench seats facing each other, once they got up in the air, he decided to switch sides and sit next to Maggie.

His move made the gondola swing, and she grabbed the railing. "What are you doing?"

"Sitting next to you. This is a much better view."

"Aren't we supposed to balance each other out?"

He liked her mix of caution and carefree, but if he had his way, he'd see her throwing caution to the wind more often. "We're fine. Look at the valley." He waved his hand toward the amazing scenery.

"It is beautiful up here," she agreed. "It's like a patchwork quilt of vineyards and grapes. I can't imagine how many dreams have started in this valley."

"And how many ended with a bad frost or a poor crop."

She made a face at him. "Okay, *Mr. Fun*, that was not an optimistic statement."

He laughed. "Sorry. I can be realistic on occasion."

As the gondola climbed the hillside, what he appreciated even more than the view was Maggie. With every breath he took, he could smell the sweetness that was her, the faint scent of citrus and flowers. He also enjoyed the shape of her bare legs, the pink nail polish on her toes, the brush of her hair against his cheek when he leaned in close. He hadn't felt so interested and connected to a woman in a very long time.

"You're crowding me, Cole," she said a little breathlessly, trying to slide away, but there was simply nowhere for her to go.

"I know. I like it."

"I don't like it." She got up and moved to the other side, giving him a pointed look.

"Why fight it, babe?"

"Fight what?"

"Me, you, us…"

"There is no us in any other way than friendship," she said firmly. "We're not even friends really. We barely know each other."

"I feel like I know quite a bit about you."

"Well, what I know about you is enough to make me sit over here."

He laughed. "What do you think is going to happen if we sit next to each other?"

"I think we're going to complicate our lives in ways neither of us want. So you stay on your side, I'll stay on mine."

"Have you always played it safe when it comes to men?"

"Now I do. I told you before that I picked every wrong guy I could find in college. I learned from my mistakes."

"Was there one wrong guy in particular?" he asked, curious to know more about her past.

She hesitated, a little pain in her blue eyes. "Yes, but I didn't think Brad was wrong at the time. In fact, I was awed by his passion for justice and civil rights. He loved to protest. I found myself walking in picket lines and chaining myself to a fence for whatever cause he was fighting. I ended up getting arrested during one of those protests. I don't think I've ever heard more disappointment in my father's voice when he found out I'd been protesting the deployment of troops into Afghanistan."

He raised an eyebrow. "You were protesting the war?"

She nodded, guilt in her expression. "So wrong, right? But my grief over my mother made me hate the Army even more. I had it in my head that if my father had been home, he would have been able to protect my mom, and she wouldn't have died. I know that wasn't a logical thought, but I couldn't shake it for a long time. When I protested the war, I was really protesting against my father and his job, his long absences, his neglect of the family—of me. It was childish and selfish, and that night in jail was a wake-up call."

"What do you mean?"

"I realized that I was letting Brad decide what I cared about, and that I was letting my anger with my dad drive me to do things I didn't really want to do. Brad didn't care for my epiphany. We split up, and that was that. Since then, I've steered away from lawbreakers and rebels with a cause."

He nodded. "I get it. You seem to me like you're often caught between two worlds, Maggie."

She raised an eyebrow. "What does that mean?"

"What you think you *should* want and what you *really* want. Who you think you *should* be and who you *really* are."

"I know who I am and what I want. Just because you don't like it—"

"I don't dislike it," he interrupted. "I just see hints of another Maggie every now and then, and I wonder if she's as eager to bury herself away in the country and always do the right thing as you are."

She stared back at him. "You've known me for two days."

"Three—if you count Friday."

"Still, you don't know me at all."

"And you haven't said I'm wrong. I'm good at reading people, Maggie. It was a skill I had to develop as a venture capitalist. I wasn't just investing in companies but in the people who ran them. I had to be able to see their true character, assess their talent, and I was great at it."

"You're modest, too. If you're so eager to analyze people, maybe you should go back to your job."

He grinned. "No need. I just analyze the people I meet on the road now. And you are one of the most interesting people I've met in a long time."

"I can't imagine what about me is so interesting," she said, shaking her head. "I'm not exciting at all. You should meet some of my friends. They put me to shame."

"I doubt that. Interesting doesn't always mean bigger than life—sometimes it just means genuine, beautiful, smart and one-of-a-kind."

She flushed a little at his words, and he suspected she didn't see herself the way he saw her.

But there was no more time for conversation. As the gondola reached the turnabout at the top of the hill, they got off and walked toward the winery.

※

Maggie was relieved to be off the gondola and away from Cole. His analysis of her had actually shaken her a little, because he had been more right than wrong. There were moments when she wondered if she were being true to herself or just trying to create the home life she'd never had. She didn't like that Cole was making her question her decisions, because she had a plan and she needed to stick to it. And why should she let him change her mind about anything anyway?

He didn't even have a job right now. He was basically living a gypsy life, and maybe he had the luxury of savings to finance his wandering travels, but she did not.

She had to worry about practical matters like bills and rent and dealing with a boss who was getting more and more ridiculously strict by the minute. Unlike Cole, she couldn't quit and just walk away. She had to make things work. While there were a lot of things she hadn't liked about her father, he had instilled in her the belief that if you started something you finished it, no matter how difficult it was.

Her dad probably wouldn't like Cole. He'd think Cole was a quitter. But was that really true? Maybe Cole should be admired for realizing his life wasn't going the way he wanted it to and taking steps to change that.

She shook the complicated thoughts out of her mind as they entered the winery. The building with its cool, red-patterned tiles on the floor, white stucco walls, dark wood ceilings and archways gave off a Spanish flair. In the tasting room, there was a long bar along one side and ceiling-to-floor windows on the other. An open door led out to a patio where circular tables topped with colorful umbrellas were set out for visitors to sit down and enjoy the view.

While Cole went to the bar to get a tasting tray, Maggie ventured over to the windows and then stepped out onto the adjacent patio to take another look at the valley in the afternoon sunshine. It was a peaceful view and the longer she stared out at the horizon, the less turbulent she felt inside. Napa was the right place for her. She could feel it down deep in her bones. No one else had to understand that but her.

"Here you are," Cole said, as he came up next to her with a tray of four small glasses of wine. "The winemaker says this is the best cabernet sauvignon and merlot they've had in years. Let's sit down."

They moved across the patio and sat down at a table. She tried the sauvignon first and it was delicious. So was the merlot. "I think these are the best wines we've tasted all day," she said.

"I agree. I wonder if the restaurant at the Stratton stocks these wines."

"I'm not sure, but if we don't, we should." She paused as one of the winemakers came out to the patio. He asked everyone to gather around, so they joined the circle of other visitors to learn more about the winery. The talk ended with a tour of the wine cellar.

"It's fascinating to me," Cole said, as they walked out of the cellar.

"What is?"

"How just about anyone in this valley with a nice piece of land can make a good wine."

"There are some very successful small wineries," she agreed. "But the industry is also big business. Napa Valley wines are sold all over the world. They compete very well with French and Italian wines."

He smiled. "You do love this valley, don't you?"

"How could you not?" she asked, sweeping her hand toward the view as they lined up for the gondola.

"I have to admit, I'm more impressed than I thought I would be. Aunt Ida has always loved Napa, but I thought that the other Stratton hotels were in far more interesting locations. I was wrong."

"Well, I'm sure Paris and London could probably beat this valley, but it depends what you're in the mood for, right? I liked living in San Francisco. I had a lot of fun with my single girlfriends for a few years, but I find I like the quiet of Napa. When I'm in San Francisco, I appreciate the city but I also feel tense with the traffic, horns honking, brakes squealing, jackhammers working on the roads, and restaurants that are so loud with conversation you can barely hear your friends talk."

"Some people find big cities energetic."

"As I said, it depends on the mood."

They boarded the gondola, and once again Cole sat next to her as they rode down. But this time she didn't bother to move. She didn't know if her relaxed buzz came from the wine or the end of a long day or just the desire to stop fighting her attraction so hard, but whatever the reason, she found herself enjoying Cole's masculine presence and didn't even protest when he put his arm around her shoulders.

They were halfway down the hillside when the gondola came to an unexpected swinging stop. She put her hand on Cole's thigh to steady herself.

"What just happened?" she asked.

"Looks like we've stopped."

"I know that, but why?"

Cole shrugged, looking completely unperturbed by the event. "No idea, but at least we have a good view while we wait to get going again."

"True, but I'd prefer it if we were still moving."

"We're fine, Maggie. We're not going to suddenly crash to the ground."

"Logically, I know that, but I can't help but notice how high up we are at the moment."

"You need to think about something else."

"Good idea. I just wish I could think of something else besides that thin cable preventing us from crashing to the group."

He smiled. "Just remember you asked."

"Asked for what?"

"Something else to think about." He pulled her toward him, covering her mouth with his as his other hand ran through her hair, holding her in place. He tasted like the wine they'd drunk earlier: hot, dizzying, delicious... She was quickly becoming addicted to the way he teased her lips apart, the slide of his tongue against her teeth, the dance of their tongues, the smell of his musky cologne. She even liked the rough edges of his shadowy beard against her cheek, the way he held her so possessively as if there was no way he was letting her go.

The last thing she wanted to do was go anywhere. She put her arms around his neck and brought his head back down after he paused to catch his breath. She didn't want air; she wanted him. She wanted to protest when his lips left hers but as he slid his mouth down the side of her neck, she shuddered with need.

Cole pulled her on to his lap so she was straddling him, so she could feel his growing hardness against her groin and all sorts of wicked thoughts ran through her. She wanted their clothes off. She wanted to explore every inch of his body and have him do the same to her. She wanted to be as bad as the bad boy she was kissing. She wanted to say yes to today and to hell with tomorrow.

And then the gondola jolted into motion again. The swinging broke them apart and the cool air that parted them put a damper on the fire that had been blazing between them.

She suddenly became very aware of where she was and what she was doing and just how far she'd let things go. She scrambled off Cole's lap and sat back in her seat, tucking her hair behind her ears, taking in one deep breath after another as she tried to slow her racing pulse.

Cole shifted somewhat uncomfortably as he ran a

hand through his hair and looked at her through desire-laden eyes. "You are something else, Maggie."

She didn't know what to say. She couldn't apologize. She couldn't pretend she hadn't just lost herself in the attraction between them. She couldn't lie about her desire. So she didn't say anything. And Cole now seemed as much at a loss for words as she was.

"That was a little too close," she said, as they neared the ground.

"I was thinking it wasn't close enough," he muttered, looking her straight in the eyes. "I want you, Maggie. I think you know that. I think you want me, too."

She drew a quick breath at the bluntness of his words, the deliberateness of his gaze. She'd never had a man state his intention in such a way. No pretty words. No fancy dinner first. No pretense. It was both refreshing and terrifying.

"Tell me I'm wrong," he commanded.

She swallowed hard, relieved she was saved from answering when the gondola came into the station. The attendant opened the door, and they got out. They walked toward the parking lot with tension now between them. She knew Cole was still waiting for an answer.

When they reached the motorcycle, she said, "Even if I want to be with you, I won't. I can't."

"Why not?"

"Because for you, I'm just a side trip, one of many stops on your endless adventure. But for me, you'd mean more."

"It doesn't have to mean more."

"It does, because I don't sleep with people I don't care about and I'm already starting to care about you, Cole. You don't want strings or an anchor, and that's exactly what I want. Tell me I'm wrong," she said, throwing his words back in his face.

He gave her a long stare. "Damn, Maggie. You know I can't tell you that."

She should have felt relief, but instead she felt disappointment. "That's what I thought. So let's just call it a day, all right?"

Before Cole could answer, her phone rang. As she took it out of her purse, she was shocked to see her father's number. "This is my father. He's calling from Germany; I have to take it."

"Of course," he said.

She walked away from the motorcycle, not really needing privacy for her call but rather a moment to catch her breath and regroup.

Chapter Seven

"Hi, Dad," she said as her father's deep baritone came over the phone. Her dad had one of those voices that naturally commanded attention, and she couldn't help straightening her shoulders as she prepared herself for whatever was about to come. Since her father called her so infrequently, she was worried that something was wrong.

"Maggie. I'm glad I caught you," he said. "I only have a few moments."

She wasn't surprised to hear that. Their conversations never lasted more than a few minutes. "Are you all right? Are Jared and Keith okay?"

"Everyone is fine as far as I know."

"Then what's going on?"

"Well, I don't know exactly how to say this, so I'll just say it—I've met someone."

His words shocked her to the core. She'd always thought her father's closest relationship was with the Army. "Are you talking about a woman?"

"Of course I am," he said impatiently.

"Who is she?"

"She's a nurse—a widow. She has a grown son." He

cleared his throat. "Her name is Helen."

"Okay," she said, not really sure what to say to his news. "Will I get to meet her at Thanksgiving?"

"Only if you come to Germany. That's why I'm calling. We won't be able to come to California for Thanksgiving."

"But I thought we were going to have a big celebration dinner at my house."

"Do you even have that house yet?"

"I'll have it by then. I really wanted to bring the family all together. Keith said he'd come for sure, and Jared is trying to make it work. Are you sure you can't come? I think it's really important for us to be together."

"Helen really wants me to meet her family, and that's the best time for them. It's just a turkey dinner, Maggie. We'll figure out another time to get the family together."

A surge of disappointment ran through her. "I was really counting on Thanksgiving."

"I didn't think it was set in stone. You can always come to Germany—I'll pay for your ticket."

And spend Thanksgiving with her father's new girlfriend and a bunch of people she'd never met before? She couldn't think of anything worse. "I don't know."

"Well, think about it. I know Helen would love to meet you. I have to run. We'll talk later."

"All right. Bye—"

The call disconnected before she could finish her sentence. That was her dad; when he was done talking, the conversation was over.

She walked back to Cole with a heavy heart. She was not just reeling from the fact that her father had once again put an end to her dream of a family holiday but also that he'd replaced her mother with a new woman.

Cole gave her a questioning look. "Are you all right? What happened?"

"I'm fine."

"You don't look fine. What's going on with your father?"

"He's in love with a woman named Helen," she said. "He can't come to my house for Thanksgiving because Helen wants him to be with her family. I asked him months ago to make sure he could come for Thanksgiving but he always changes the plans. It doesn't matter what I want, only what he wants."

"Sorry," Cole said, genuine compassion in his eyes.

"I shouldn't be surprised. It's always been this way. If I don't go to my dad, I don't see him."

"That sucks."

She appreciated that Cole didn't try to make excuses for her father. "It does. Hopefully, my brothers will still come, unless my dad talks them into going to Germany, which is a definite possibility."

"Maybe you should consider joining them."

"I don't want to meet his new girlfriend. I don't want to be nice to a bunch of strangers," she said grumpily.

"Well, you don't have to decide right now, do you?"

"No, that's true."

"You know what you need?" Cole asked.

She gave him a suspicious look. "If the answer is sex or more wine, I'm going to say no."

He laughed. "Don't knock sex and wine. They can cure a lot of heartache."

"Or cause more," she said cynically.

"Well, I was actually talking about something else."

"What?"

"I'll surprise you."

"I'd rather just know where we're going."

"So you can come up with a dozen reasons why not?"

"That sounds like we're going someplace I definitely don't want to go."

He handed over her helmet. "Sometimes you just have to enjoy the ride and not worry about the destination. If you don't like it when we get there, we'll leave. Deal?"

"Deal," she said, getting onto the bike behind him.

She was actually happy to leave the driving and decisions to him for a few moments. She needed to breathe through the pain of the blow her father had just delivered. She should try to find a way to be happy for him. It wasn't good for anyone to be alone, but somehow it still stung a little. He wasn't just getting involved with a woman; he was choosing her and her family over his own. But Maggie was quite sure he didn't see it that way. In fact, he'd probably hung up the phone thinking she was being unreasonable as usual.

As Cole drove them down the highway, she tried to let the bad feelings go. She had a lot to be happy about. She couldn't let her father take her down. He'd ruined too many of her holidays already. She'd make Thanksgiving work whether he was there or not.

Cole took a curve a little faster than she would have liked, but she wasn't afraid. She'd somehow come to trust him. It was way too fast, and she was probably crazy to put her faith in someone she'd known a few days but deep down in her gut she knew that Cole was someone she could depend on. Still, she tightened her arms around him, happy to have a reason to hold onto him, because as soon as they got off the bike, she was going to let him go.

Thirty minutes later, Cole drove through the downtown area, stopping in front of Schaeffer's Ice-Cream Parlor and Candy Shop.

As they got off the bike, Cole said, "What do you think of my idea now?"

"It's the best one you've had all day. I love Schaeffer's ice cream. They make it from scratch in the back."

"That's what I hear. You look better now, Maggie; the color is back in your face."

"Thanks to the sun and wind."

"You liked the bike ride more than you thought you would, didn't you?"

"Maybe, but my expectations were very low. They tend to stay in that range when it comes to motorcycles and men."

He grinned. "I'll have to see what I can do to raise those expectations."

"That wasn't a challenge."

"Too late. I've already taken it that way."

"Fine. You can start impressing me by buying me a double scoop of ice cream."

"You're on." He opened the door and ushered her inside.

The ice-cream parlor and candy store was a pink and white confection of sugar and sweets. Pete Schaeffer and his wife Lily worked the ice cream counter while their two high school daughters were behind the candy counter.

Pete and Lily were two of Maggie's favorite people. They were both in their late forties and had been married for eighteen years. They'd left their other jobs to open their dream of a business two years earlier and the parlor was quickly becoming one of Napa's favorite stops.

"Hi, Maggie," Pete said with a friendly grin. He had thinning brown hair and an engaging pair of dark eyes.

"Hi, Pete—Lily," she added, waving to the woman who was finishing up with another customer.

"What are you going for today?" Pete asked. "Triple decker banana split?"

"Not today."

"Wait—is that what you usually order?" Cole interrupted with surprise in his eyes.

"It's a house specialty. I've tried it a few times."

"Like just about every time," Pete corrected. "Maggie can put it away."

"You don't need to tell him that, Pete," Lily interrupted. "Maggie doesn't want her date to know all her secrets, do you dear?"

"He's not my date. He's just..." She couldn't think of the right word, so she said, "He's Mrs. Stratton's nephew."

"Great to meet you," Pete said, reaching across the counter to shake Cole's hand. "Your aunt is a classy lady."

"The Stratton buys a lot of ice cream from this store," Maggie put in.

"So today, whatever you want is on the house," Pete added.

"I'll take a double scoop of mint chip," she said.

"I'll go with a double chocolate mocha," Cole said.

"Coming right up," Pete replied.

"This place is amazing," Cole said. "I feel like I'm in the middle of a giant swirl of cotton candy."

She laughed. "I feel like I gain five pounds every time I walk in here, which you've probably surmised is way too much."

"I'm an ice cream fan, too," he confessed. "My favorite dessert."

"I love to hear that," Peter said, interrupting their conversation to hand Maggie her cup of mint chip. "Don't be a stranger while you're in town."

"I'm sure I won't be," Cole promised.

"This place was Pete and Lily's dream business," Maggie said, as Lily handed Cole his order.

"That's right," Lily said, putting her arm around her husband's waist. "Pete and I met in an ice-cream shop near our college dorms. We were both ice cream addicts. That first year we made a goal to try every single flavor. Along the way, we fell in love and made a promise that one day we'd open our own place. It took us twenty years, but it finally happened, which just goes to show that some dreams take a little longer, but as long as you don't quit, you can't fail."

"I admire your commitment," Cole said.

"Enjoy your ice cream," Lily told them.

They sat down at a table by the window as more customers flooded into the store.

"What did you think of their story?" Maggie asked him as she spooned ice cream into her mouth.

"It sounds like one of those romance novel plots my mom likes to read."

She smiled. "Your mom reads romance novels?"

"I think a more appropriate word than read would be devour. She used to have hundreds of books in our house. Now she puts them on her tablet. But whenever she isn't painting, she usually has her nose in a book."

"Are you a reader?"

"I used to read the financial pages from cover to cover. Now, I read maps. I plot out places I want to go. I don't want to read about them. I want to see them for myself."

There was a certain romance to his life, she thought. But she wondered how long it would take for him to feel a longing for a home-cooked meal and a place to call home. "Where will you go when you leave here?"

"I'm not sure yet. I'm thinking about Hawaii. It's been years since I've done any island living. Have you been there?"

"I went to Maui for a week when I was in college. It was beautiful. I'd love to go back some time or maybe try one of the other islands. And now I'd spend more time touring the island and less time sunbathing and looking for cute guys," she added with a self-deprecating smile.

He grinned. "I'm sure they were looking right back."

"And probably having a difficult time seeing beyond my massive sunburn. I cooked myself to a crisp in about an hour the first day I was there. After that, I was coating myself with sunscreen and wearing long sleeves and long dresses."

"You have beautiful but very fair skin."

She flushed a little at the appreciation in his eyes. "I wouldn't call my skin tone beautiful. I'm pale and I freckle easily."

"You only see your flaws; I see so much more."

She wanted to ask him what else he saw, but that would probably sound like she was begging for compliments. "How long will you be in Hawaii?"

He shrugged. "I have no plans."

"Really? Even though it sounds fun to have no plans, I don't think I could live with such a lack of structure."

"It took me a while to unplug from technology, to not feel like I was idling the day away. Years of stress and work habits don't disappear overnight, but then one day you wake up and you feel happy just to see an amazing sunset or walk on a deserted beach."

"You're very convincing, but I don't know…there's something that doesn't quite add up."

"What do you mean?"

"I just have a gut feeling that you're not as much of a beach bum as you'd like me to believe."

"You think I have a secret life?"

"Do you?"

He smiled. "You have a big imagination."

"Well, that's true." She paused. "Ice cream was a good idea. I feel better."

"Good. So what are you doing tonight, Maggie?"

"I thought I'd try baking another apple pie. I have to get it right sometime. What about you? You don't appear to be spending much time with your aunt."

"She is taking me to dinner at some highbrow place that apparently requires a coat and tie," he said with a sigh.

She smiled at the look of distaste on his face. "Oh, the horrors."

"I used to love wearing a good suit, but now a tie just feels like it's choking me."

"I'm sure the food will be worth a little discomfort. I wonder if she's taking you to Echo—it's a new restaurant in town, very chic and very expensive."

"I told her I'd be happy with a burger somewhere, but she said she wants to treat me to something special. I have a hard time saying no to Aunt Ida."

"Me, too. That's how I ended up with you yesterday."

He grinned. "And me with you. But I'm glad she hooked us up. I had fun today, Maggie. I hope you did, too."

"I did," she said softly, meeting his gaze. "But I

should probably go home now."

"I guess it is that time. I just don't really want to say good-bye to you."

Her stomach flipped over at his words and the look in his eyes. "I don't think it's good-bye, is it? You're not leaving for another week; I'm sure we'll see each other again."

"You won't be trying to avoid me?"

"I can't promise that," she admitted.

"That's what I was afraid of. You have a habit of letting yourself go and then pulling yourself back just as quickly."

"So I don't fall," she said.

"Maybe you wouldn't fall; maybe you'd fly. But you don't give yourself a chance to find out."

"Someday—maybe I'll do that."

"But not today."

She shook her head. "Not today." Today, she was playing it safe.

Chapter Eight

Monday morning, Maggie woke up after a couple hours of sleep with a headache that she blamed completely on Cole. Although she hadn't seen him or heard from him since he'd dropped her off Sunday afternoon, he'd been in her head ever since he'd said goodbye—a goodbye that had come without a kiss—a fact she should have been happy about but somehow wasn't.

Shaking that disturbing thought out of her head, she showered, dressed in jeans and a knit top, and mentally planned out her day. The Cougars' playoff game started at three, so she needed to leave her house by eleven to get to San Francisco in plenty of time for the first pitch. Since it was only nine, she had two hours to get something done. Since she'd been too tired to bake the night before, she'd give her apple pie another shot this morning. The Harvest Festival opened on Wednesday, so she was running out of time to come up with the right recipe. She should probably just give up, but it wasn't in her nature to quit.

As she headed into the kitchen, her phone rang; it was her brother Keith on the line.

"Hi, Keith. How are you?"

"Good. And you?"

"Not bad. Where are you?"

"Can't say."

"But you're safe?" She didn't know why she always asked that question, because neither her father nor her brothers ever gave her a straight answer, but she couldn't help worrying about them.

"I'm talking on the phone to you, so yeah I'm safe. What's going on in Napa?"

"The Harvest Festival is coming up. I've grown a pumpkin that is over a hundred pounds."

"Seriously? Why did you do that?"

"Because I have a garden, and I had pumpkin seeds, and I thought it would be fun. Don't you remember all the state fairs Mom used to take us to? She always talked about growing a pumpkin and entering it in the contest."

"I don't remember the pumpkins, but I do remember her apple pie."

"I'm trying to make one of those, too, but so far I haven't been successful. I swear there's some secret ingredient she put in there. Do you know what it was?"

"Are you kidding? I stayed as far away from the kitchen as I could. Don't you have better things to do than to grow pumpkins and make pies? Like your job?"

"I go to work every day. The other stuff is just on the side. The Stratton is great. I love working there. Well, that's not completely true. My boss has got some stick up his ass these days and is making my life a little miserable. I don't know if he's going through a midlife crisis or what, but he's definitely become super critical."

"That sucks, but sometimes it's good to have someone pushing you to be the best."

"I don't know if that's what he's pushing me to be. Sometimes I think he's trying to push me out of the hotel."

"Well, don't let him."

Things were always very black-and-white where Keith was concerned. "I'm glad you called, because I wanted to talk to you about Thanksgiving."

"Yeah, about that," he said, a heavy note in his voice.

She sat down on the stool by her kitchen island, dreading what was coming next. "Don't tell me you're not coming, Keith. You know I'm planning a big celebration."

"I don't think I can make it, Maggie. I'll have a better chance getting to Germany. I'm probably only going to have two days off. Why don't you come there?"

"So I can hang out with Dad's new girlfriend?"

"She's not bad."

"You already met her?" she asked in shock. "I just heard about her yesterday."

"Dad wasn't sure how to tell you. He knows how close you and Mom were."

"How long has it been going on?"

"I'm not sure—a few months maybe. Why don't you come to Germany? If you need help on the ticket, I'll send you some money."

"It's not just the money. I usually have to work at least one day on the holiday weekend, and I really wanted to show everyone my house. I wanted to cook dinner and sit around the table the way we used to."

"Let's shoot for Christmas then."

"All right," she said with a sigh, having a feeling that Christmas would be an even longer shot than Thanksgiving. "Stay safe, Keith."

"I will. And think about coming to Germany. We'll talk soon."

She set the phone down on the kitchen counter and felt another wave of disappointment run through her. It was possible she could still get her other brother to Napa for Thanksgiving, but the way things were going she suspected he'd probably go to Germany, too. The three men in her family had always been extremely close, and she'd always felt a little left out. They loved her, of course, but they didn't have as much in common with her as they did with each other.

The sharp peal of the doorbell sent a tingle of anticipation down her spine. It could be anyone, but she couldn't help taking a quick peek in the hall mirror on her way to answer the door.

Cole gave her a smile when she opened the door. "Hey, how's it going?"

"Fine. What are you doing here?"

"I wanted to say thank you, and you never gave me your number."

"What are you thanking me for?"

"Showing me around town, touring the wineries with me," he replied with a smile. He held up a shopping bag. "And I come bearing gifts."

"What kind of gifts?"

"Apples, flour, cinnamon, sugar and a few other things."

"That sounds like the ingredients for a pie."

"I thought we could make one together."

"You're going to bake a pie with me?" she asked doubtfully. "Really? Why?"

"So I can do more than just say thank you. Are you going to let me in?"

"Maybe, but I think we should get something straight."

He grinned. "You don't have to say it."

"Are you sure I don't have to say it?"

"Yes. You're not going to have sex with me just because I help you bake a pie. There, I said it. Really, Maggie, do you think I'm that shady?"

She didn't think he was shady, but she also didn't think his motive was as altruistic as he said it was. "All right, come on in. I was actually just about to get started on my own pie," she added as they walked down the hall.

"Maybe we should each make a pie and see which is better," he said.

"You like to compete, don't you?"

"It might make it more fun."

"Great."

He set his bag of groceries on the counter and looked around the kitchen. "I'll work over by the sink; you can work here. No peeking."

"You think I'm going to steal your recipe?" she asked.

He smiled. "I think you probably should steal my recipe."

She made a face at him. "Where did you get your recipe?"

"My grandmother used to make pies for the holidays."

"I thought you were estranged from your family."

"Not my grandmother on the Stratton side; my grandmother on my father's side. She was a lovely person and she liked to bake Sometimes I helped her."

"I can't picture you in a kitchen with an apron." Even as she said the words, a sexy image of Cole wearing nothing but an apron flashed through her mind, and she felt the heat warm her cheeks.

He laughed. "You are bad, Maggie."

"You have no idea what I'm thinking."

"Oh, I'm pretty sure I do."

"Let's just concentrate on pie."

"You're on."

For the next half hour, they made pie filling and crust. While she did try to sneak a peek at what Cole was doing, she couldn't really see anything. Not that she wanted to copy him, but she was curious to see what he was putting into the pie. She also enjoyed watching him roll out flour dough, cut up apples, and measure spices. She'd never had a man cook with her or for her, and it was more appealing than she ever would have imagined.

As beads of sweat dotted her forehead, she realized it wasn't just the oven that was preheating; it was also her. She forced herself to look away from Cole and stop imagining his hands molding her curves the way he was lovingly shaping his pie dough.

She smiled at that wicked thought, then got back to work.

Finally, both pies were ready to bake. They put them next to each other in the oven and set the timer.

"Yours did look pretty," Maggie said grudgingly.

"So did yours. But we both know, the truth is in the filling." He wiped his floury hands on a towel. "Do you mind if I grab a cup of coffee?"

"Of course not." She opened the cupboard and pulled out a mug.

As he filled it up, she said, "How was the restaurant last night? Did your aunt take you to Echo?"

"She did, and it was as you described," he said, sliding onto a stool by the island. "Luxurious dining room, pretentious waiters, and excellent food."

"How was your aunt?"

"She was in good spirits, but then Aunt Ida rarely lets

herself get down about anything. She's always got a smile on her face."

"I've noticed that."

"She hasn't always had an easy life, either. Her husband was sick for almost eight years before he died of cancer five years ago. She spent a lot of time taking care of him, but she never complained. She adored him."

"They didn't have any children, did they?"

"No. Ida said she never wanted kids. She likes being an aunt, and she has thirteen nieces and nephews, so she gets a lot of practice." He paused. "We were all a little worried about her after her husband died. She seemed at loose ends for a long time. Last year she decided to spend several months traveling, and I think it was really good for her. She seems more like her old self now."

"I'm glad she had a good time, but we missed having her around the hotel. I think things always run more smoothly when she's there."

"Harry Stone doesn't keep things running smoothly?"

"He keeps things running, but he is very rigid and inflexible, and as I mentioned before he's become difficult to work with the last few months. He's like a powder keg. Just about anything can set him off, and I seem to be the one who pushes most of his buttons. I'm good at my job," she added, wanting there to be no mistake about that. "I get along well with our guests. But sometimes, I go the extra mile, and it's not a mile Mr. Stone wants me to go."

"Like what?"

"Mrs. Kensington's dog, for one."

He raised an eyebrow. "What happened?"

"Mrs. Kensington had a poodle that she treated like a son. This dog lived better than I do. He was supposed to stay with her sister, but then her sister got sick, and she needed to have the dog stay at the hotel with her. She comes to the hotel every year and spends a lot of money there, so I wanted to make sure she was happy. Plus, it was her eighty-fifth birthday, and except for her sister, Strauss—that was the name of her poodle—is her only family."

"What did you do?"

"I snuck the dog into the hotel. I didn't think one night would make that much difference. I was going to personally clean the room after she left and if there was any damage to the carpet, I was going to pay for it."

"I'm betting you got caught."

"Yes, but I was so close... I had the dog stashed under a food-service table, and I told the other clerk at the desk that I was going to make a personal room service delivery. I picked up Mrs. Kensington's favorite roasted chicken dinner from the restaurant, and I made it into the elevator with no problem. And then what happens? The elevator gets stuck. The dog and I were in there for twenty minutes. I can't control him. He eats all the food on the table. Then he has an accident on the floor."

Cole grinned. "That's pretty funny, Maggie."

"Mr. Stone was not amused. He wouldn't have known except Mrs. Kensington freaked out when I didn't appear with her precious dog and she told everyone in the world that her dog was stuck in the elevator. So when the doors opened, everyone was waiting for me. I got written up for what I did, but I was really just trying to help an old, lonely woman."

"Your heart was in the right place."

"That didn't matter. And you know what—Mrs. Kensington turned on me, too. She got mad at me for letting Strauss eat the chicken, as if I could have stopped him. He was a little biter. When I got too close, he tried to bite my hand."

Cole started laughing. "I can see it so clearly."

"It really wasn't that funny."

"It sounds like it was. Maybe you should think of working at another hotel where the management is less restrictive."

"No way. I love the Stratton, and I need three more paychecks to make my down payment, so I am going to do everything I can to stay on Mr. Stone's good side for the next six weeks." She sipped her coffee. "Tell me more about your previous job as a venture capitalist. What kind of ventures did you invest in?"

"A lot of them were technology based. It wasn't very exciting and certainly not as entertaining as your dog story."

"But I'm guessing it was lucrative," she ventured. "Obviously, you're able to finance your gypsy lifestyle with your savings—unless it's with family money."

"I don't take money from my family," he said flatly. "And, yes, I made a lot of cash with the firm, but I never had time to spend it. Now I do have time, but I find myself living fairly simply. I don't need a lot."

"Lucky you."

"I am lucky," he said, meeting her gaze. "I was able to take control of my life and not live according to someone else's expectations."

"Sometimes expectations are good; they make you try harder."

"I can motivate myself; I think you can, too. You haven't given up on your pie."

"Well, not yet, but this might be my last attempt. I'm running out of time and hope." She picked up her phone as a text came in. It was from her other brother. She read it quickly and let out a sigh. "Well, the family mutiny is now complete. I talked to one brother earlier; he's going to Germany for Thanksgiving, and now my other brother is going to join him and my dad."

"You could go, too."

"I usually have to work part of that weekend."

"If you wanted to get off, don't you think you could?"

"I don't know—maybe. But I'm a little tired of being in a family that only wants to see me on their terms. That probably sounds childish, but it's how I feel."

Understanding filled Cole's eyes. "No, I get it. But speaking as a man who knows something about how men think, I have to ask you if you've ever talked to your father or your brothers about how you feel."

She sighed. "You don't talk to my dad about feelings. He only wants to hear plans or achievements."

"You should try to get past that wall."

"He's never been the kind of father I could talk to about personal things."

"He still could be. Sometimes you have to tell us exactly what's going on and don't expect us to guess. My gender is not good at guessing what women think and want. Your father and brothers may have no idea how unhappy you are."

"I did tell them I wanted them to come here."

"So, tell them again and again until they hear you."

"How can I do that, Cole? My brothers and my father are serving our country. They're risking their lives every day. They're heroes. Why shouldn't they have the holiday where they want it? What am I doing that's so important?"

"Maggie, stop."

"What?"

"Stop putting yourself down."

"Why? I'm just being honest. I don't save lives in my job. And my spare time isn't spent saving the world, that's for sure."

"You make people happy, Maggie. You give them your attention. You make them feel special and important. And if you enjoy baking and gardening, good for you. Someone is going to enjoy your gigantic pumpkin and hopefully your pie as well."

She smiled. "That's a nice thing to say. I'm sorry, Cole. I don't know why I keep dumping my family problems on you. I'm not usually this talkative, especially with someone I don't know that well."

"You don't have to apologize. I like our talks. I'm going to miss them when I go."

She was going to miss them, too. "You know, I think you're more intuitive than you think when it comes to women. You always seem to make me feel better."

"I'm glad, but I'm definitely a work in progress."

She liked his admission. She liked *him*. She just didn't know what to do about it. She got up and turned on the oven light so she could see the pies. They were cooking nicely. She glanced at the oven timer. "We have about five more minutes until the pies are done."

"What should we do in the meantime?" he asked, getting to his feet.

She saw the wicked light in his eyes. "Not that."

"Not what?"

"I can read your mind, Cole."

He stepped forward and put his arms around her. "Do you know how long it's been since I kissed you?"

"Too long?" she answered with a breathless sigh of desire.

"Exactly. Way too long."

"Then kiss me," she said, breaching the distance between them.

Their lips touched together in steamy heat and as she moved into his arms, it felt so completely and utterly right. She closed her eyes and opened her mouth and enjoyed every swipe of his tongue, every warm corner of his mouth, every tiny escape of his breath as desire rose between them. She ran her hands up under his shirt. His body was muscled, hard and powerful, and she was very aware of how different they were and yet how perfectly they fit together. She was also aware of just how alone they were, how close her bedroom was, how easy it would be to take him down the hall.

And then the oven timer went off.

They broke apart, and she immediately moved toward the oven. "They're done." She took the pies out and set them side-by-side on the cooling rack. "They look good," she said, still feeling a little dazed from Cole's kiss.

"You look good, Maggie," Cole said, staring back at her.

"Cole, we can't. I told you that before you came in the house."

"I know, but you just reminded me how good we are together."

"You're leaving in a few days."

"I am, but if I've learned anything in the last few years, it's that you shouldn't put off having what you really want."

"Spoken like a man who's leaving soon." As she finished speaking, her phone dinged. "I should look at that."

"Of course you should," he said with a sigh. "I think the universe is conspiring against me. What's going to go off next—the doorbell?"

She moved down the counter to get her phone. The text was from Julie, letting her know that Andrea couldn't make the game, so she had an extra ticket if Maggie wanted to bring someone.

The text sent her gaze back to Cole, and another really bad idea entered her head. *But it wasn't as bad as going to bed with him, right?*

"Are you free today, Cole?"

"I'm supposed to meet my aunt later, but why do you ask?"

"My friend Julie's fiancé plays for the San Francisco Cougars. They're in the playoffs, and they have a home game this afternoon. She has an extra ticket and said I can bring someone if I want to. Would you want to go to a baseball game?"

"A Cougars' playoff game? Hell, yes."

The excitement in his eyes made her smile. "Okay, good. The seats will be amazing, I'm sure."

"I don't care if they're in the last row of the outfield."

"Since Julie's fiancé is Matt Kingsley, I can guarantee the seats will be better than that."

"Matt Kingsley? Seriously? The guy hit over .400 this season."

"You follow the Cougars?"

"I follow the good players, and he is one of the best. Did I say yes yet?"

"Not officially, but I can tell that you are in."

"All in. What time do we leave?"

She glanced at the clock. "About an hour. That should give us plenty of time to get to the city. I'm driving, by the way. No motorcycle trips to San Francisco for me."

"You got it. I just need to call my aunt and tell her I'll meet her later."

"Will she be upset?"

"If I tell her I'm with you, I doubt it. I'll be right back."

"Okay," she said, wondering why he felt the need to make the call in private, but since she could use a few minutes away from him, she let him go without comment.

She picked up her phone and smiled as she texted Julie: "*Going to bring a hot, single guy with me then.*"

Julie's answer came back almost immediately. "*Who is he?*"

"*You'll meet him when we get there.*"

Maggie smiled to herself. That should keep her girlfriends guessing for a while.

Chapter Nine

"I'm not going to be able to spend time in the hotel office today," Cole told his aunt as he stepped on to Maggie's porch. "I'm sorry, but something has come up." He knew he was letting her down, but there was no way he wasn't going to the game with Maggie. It was the playoffs. And it was with Maggie. He wasn't actually sure which he found more irresistible.

"Really?" Ida said, disappointment in her voice. "But Mr. Stone is gone today, Cole. It's the perfect time for you to snoop around the office."

"I know. I'll do it tonight. He won't be back in the office until tomorrow morning, right?"

"I guess that will work. I hope whatever came up is good," she added.

"It's very good. I have the opportunity to go to the Cougars' playoff game in San Francisco."

"Well, that sounds like fun. You know, Maggie's friend is marrying someone on the Cougars."

"I just found that out."

"So you're going with Maggie. How did that happen? I thought you weren't going to see her again."

"I'll tell you later. I have to go now."

"Say hello to Maggie for me."

He slipped his phone into his pocket and went back into the house.

"Everything okay?" Maggie asked, curiosity in her blue eyes.

"All good. So, I think we're ready for the moment of truth."

She drew in a deep breath. "Yes, it's time for pie. I really, really hope mine is better than yours."

He grinned. "I feel the same way." As soon as the words left his mouth, he realized he didn't actually feel that way at all, because beating Maggie was probably going to put disappointment in her beautiful gaze, and he hated to be the one to make her feel bad. But it was too late to call off the contest.

Maggie grabbed four small plates from the cupboard. She cut two pieces from each pie so that they could each taste both pies and handed him a fork. "Let's try yours first," she said.

He scooped up a large bite of his pie, happy that the crust was crisp, the apples were soft and warm, and there was the perfect blend of sugar and cinnamon. He swallowed, watching Maggie's thoughtful expression as she ate his pie.

She let out a sigh. "Well, that was…"

"Good?" he suggested.

"Amazing," she admitted. "Maybe the best apple pie I've ever had."

"We haven't tried yours yet."

"I can't imagine my pie is going to beat this one."

"Let's find out." He tried Maggie's pie, happier that it wasn't as bad as the last pie he'd tasted, but the apples were a little too crunchy and there was some odd flavor that just didn't blend well with the fruit.

Maggie swallowed her bite, then took her plate over to the garbage and dumped it into the trash.

"It's not that bad," he said.

"Don't lie. It's terrible. Why were your apples more done than mine? They cooked for the same amount of time."

"I cut the slices smaller, and I used a different brand of apple that was juicier. Did you add something besides cinnamon and sugar to the filling? There's a taste I can't place."

"I added some caramel to the filling and some oats to the pie crust."

Which explained why the crust tasted off, too. "Why don't you use my recipe, Maggie? I can show you how to make it."

"But then it won't be mine—it will be yours."

The keen disappointment in her voice told him her emotional reaction was about more than a pie. "What's this really about, Maggie? Because I know it's not about pie. Is it about your mom?"

"Yes. I want to keep some of my mom's traditions alive, but I can't seem to do that. I wish I'd paid more attention when she was baking. I wish I'd asked her more questions. I should have been more willing to let her teach me what she knew."

"So, you feel guilty about the time you didn't spend with your mom."

"I was a selfish kid. I took her for granted."

"Every kid does that. You told me you and your mom were close."

"We were close but obviously not close enough, because I can't make her damn pie." She furiously blinked the moisture from her eyes.

"I know that I can't talk you out of feeling guilty, Maggie, but I have to say that I don't believe your mother's dream for you was to be able to make her apple pie. I'm sure she wanted you to have your own dreams, to be yourself, not her. Don't make the pie more important than it is. If you can't replicate it, so what? You probably do a lot of things better than her." As he finished speaking, he realized he hadn't felt so determined to make someone feel better than he did right now. He also hadn't gotten this involved in someone else's personal business in a very long time—if ever.

"You're right, Cole. My mom always wanted me to reach for the stars. She wouldn't care that I couldn't make a pie. In fact, she knew I was pretty bad at baking. Why am I trying to honor her memory by pretending to be her? I need to be me."

"That's what I'm saying."

"It all began when I moved out of the city and into this house. I started thinking about settling down, making a home for the rest of my family the way my mom did." She met his gaze. "And for some reason, I missed her more when I got here, maybe because I didn't have any roommates to distract me, and because my dad and brothers are so far away."

"You're always going to miss her. Just don't keep kicking yourself for not being the perfect kid, because no child is perfect. I certainly wasn't. And I'm betting your brothers weren't, either."

"They were far from perfect," she said with a roll of her eyes. "But they do honor my dad's legacy by following in his footsteps. I guess I was trying to follow in my mom's footsteps, but we just aren't good at the same things." She drew in a breath and let it out. "Okay, I'm done with the pie."

"Hallelujah."

She smiled. "But I'm still taking the pumpkin to the Harvest Festival. I didn't spend all summer babysitting that pumpkin for nothing."

"You should do whatever *you* want to do—that's the point."

"Thanks, Cole. I must admit, I really didn't think you were going to be the person to hold a mirror up for me to look into."

"I'm not usually the person who does that, but here we are."

"Here we are," she echoed.

The air crackled between them. He wanted to kiss her again. And he was even tempted to say to hell with the playoffs if he could take her to bed, but she was already talking again.

"We should get going," she said. "There could be a lot of traffic heading into the city. I'm going to grab a sweater and change my top. Do you need to stop by the hotel?"

"No, I'm good. I'll clean up in here."

"I can do that later."

"Go," he said, waving her away. "It's the least I can do."

She paused in the doorway. "You've done a lot more than you might think."

"It's easier to see what other people are doing wrong."

"Well, maybe someday I can return the favor and hold up a mirror for you to look into."

"I hope not," he said somewhat fervently.

She laughed. "Better at dishing it out than taking it?"

"You know it."

He smiled to himself as she left the room, and as he rinsed the plates and set them in the dishwasher, he couldn't help thinking that Maggie's charming little cottage felt more like a home than the mansion he used to live in. But he couldn't get too comfortable. He was done with home ownership, lawns that needed mowing, rooms that needed decorating, mortgages that needed paying. Maggie might want all that, but he didn't, and he couldn't forget that.

—•➤➤◀◀•—

The drive to the San Francisco ballpark took about an hour and a half with only the Bay Bridge traffic slowing them down. On the way, Cole entertained Maggie with tales from the road. He'd definitely been a lot of interesting places over the past few years, and he had met some crazy people. One thing she was beginning to realize about Cole was that he'd didn't just travel and observe; he participated. He talked to people because he was genuinely interested in their lives.

"You have something in common with your aunt," she said, as they drove into the parking lot at the ballpark.

"What's that?"

"You like to get to know people for who they are. She always makes a point of talking to the staff, asking them questions, learning about their families. It makes her feel like a friend, not just a boss, and you do the same thing."

"I didn't for a long time. I was caught up in spreadsheets and profit and loss estimations. The part I enjoyed most about being a venture capitalist was being able to make someone's dream a reality, but that was about fifteen percent of my job, and the rest was cold-blooded analysis. Although I rose high within the firm, I didn't have the final say, and sometimes the people I wanted to fund I couldn't."

"That must have been disappointing."

"It's always disappointing when you can't convince someone of your point of view."

"Very true. Looks like a big crowd," she added, as she slowly maneuvered her way through the crowded lot.

"Big game today," he said, a light of excitement in his eyes.

"You look pretty happy to be here."

"There's nothing better than a playoff game. Do you know Kingsley pretty well?"

"Well enough. He's a great guy, very down-to-earth, not at all cocky. And he treats Julie like she's gold. I'm so glad they found each other. It was a little rough at first, because Julie's dad was a ballplayer and he wasn't a great family man, so Julie wasn't sure she wanted to give Matt a chance. But he persuaded her to do so, and they're getting married in December. I will be a bridesmaid for the fourth time in a year and a half."

"Seriously? That's a lot."

"And there's no end in sight. One of my other friends, Isabella, just got engaged, so that will be number five. I don't think she's set a date yet, but it will probably be around Valentine's Day. I was part of a really close group of friends in college. We met freshman year in the dorms. After graduation, we vowed that we would stay in touch, and no matter where we were, we'd stand up for each other in our weddings."

"How many are in the group?"

"Eight including me, so that will be seven bridesmaids dresses."

"Hope you're saving some of your paychecks for weddings."

"I am. It does get expensive, but I love my friends. I want to be there for them on an important day in their lives. You'll get to meet a couple of them today. Along with Julie who will, of course, be there to root on her soon-to-be husband, Liz is coming with her husband Michael, and Kate and Jessica will be there, along with Jessica's seven-year-old son Brandon."

"Sounds like a crowd. What can you tell me about the others?"

"Liz is in public relations with her husband Michael Stafford. Michael used to play football before he had to retire due to an injury."

Cole raised an eyebrow. "Another pro athlete?"

She smiled. "Yes, but Liz and Michael actually fell in love in high school; they just didn't realize it until they met up again last year. Then there's Kate. She's a wedding planner and single. She lives in San Francisco. Jessica is a teacher and lives in San Diego, but she's apparently thinking of coming back to the Bay Area. She's a single mom. She married her college boyfriend in a civil ceremony our senior year, and none of us were in the wedding. You can say it's a coincidence…but she got divorced a year later."

"I could also say it was a case of being too young," he said dryly.

"That, too," she agreed. "Anyway, after we all missed her wedding, we made the agreement not to let that happen again. Hopefully, Jessica will get married again someday and we can do it right." She pulled into a spot, and they got out of the car.

As they walked toward the ballpark, Cole slipped his hand into hers, and she liked his warm grip a lot. She couldn't remember the last time she'd held hands with a man. It was such a simple thing and yet it felt intimate, as if she and Cole were alone in the middle of the huge crowd. Only, she wasn't alone. She had a gorgeous man walking with her.

But for how long?

She shoved the question aside. Today she was going to live in the moment and not worry about tomorrow.

Chapter Ten

—➤➤◄◄◄—

Cole squeezed Maggie's fingers as they made their way through security and into the ballpark. The stadium was packed, and the atmosphere was energized. He hadn't been to a baseball game in a while, and he was excited to be part of the playoff action.

The San Francisco Stadium was only five years old, so he'd never been inside, and he had to admit he was impressed by the layout of the seats set close to the action and the views out to centerfield and the San Francisco Bay beyond.

Maggie led him down to a box of eight seats just behind the home team dugout. Two pretty blondes and a rugged-looking male greeted them.

After Maggie hugged her friends, she made the introductions. "This is Julie, Matt's fiancée, and Liz and Michael Stafford. This is Cole Hastings."

"Nice to meet you," he said, shaking hands with Michael and smiling at the women.

"Hey, don't leave us out," a dark-haired, dark-eyed woman interrupted.

"Sorry, I didn't see you guys," Maggie said, stepping into the aisle to greet the new arrival and her son. "Cole, this is Jessica and her son Brandon. This is my friend Cole Hastings."

"Jessica, Brandon," he echoed, very aware that Maggie's friends were giving him the once-over. That was fine. He liked protective friends, especially where Maggie was concerned. She might be a little too friendly and trusting for her own good.

"I'm so glad you could all come," Julie said. "These games are getting so stressful for me. I need some friendly distractions, or I'll bite my nails down to the quick."

"We're here for you," Maggie said.

"Who wants food and drinks?" Michael asked. "I'm going to make a snack bar run."

"I'm good," Julie said. "I'll eat later when the Cougars have a comfortable lead and Matt has had a couple of good at bats."

Maggie looked at Cole. "Are you hungry?"

"Starving. How about you?"

"I would love a hot dog and garlic fries."

He laughed. "A girl after my own heart."

She smiled. "Sometimes I have the diet of a twelve-year-old."

"Me, too. I'll go with Michael," he said.

"Thanks."

Cole followed Michael up to the snack bar where they found a very long line. "So how do you know Maggie?" Michael asked as they settled in for a wait.

"We met a few days ago. My aunt owns the hotel where she works—the Stratton."

"I love the Stratton. Liz and I got married there. We had our reception in the garden. It was wonderful. Your aunt is Ida Stratton?"

"Yes."

"She was amazing. She gave us a free room and sent champagne and chocolates to us just because we were Maggie's friends."

"That sounds like my aunt. She's very generous, and she loves love and weddings."

"What woman doesn't?" Michael asked with a laugh. "Liz's friends are starting to make a lot of trips down the aisle. Every time we get together we're talking about someone's wedding plans."

"Maggie mentioned that she's in a lot of weddings these days."

"They're a tight group. So, are you in the hotel business?"

"I wasn't planning to be, but things seem to be going in that direction. My family owns several hotels, and I've been doing some consulting work for them while I figure out where I want my career to go next." He wasn't as vague with Michael as he'd been with Maggie. He didn't want the guy to think he was a freeloading loser.

"Changing careers is stressful," Michael said with a nod. "I transitioned from professional football to public relations, and now I have a foot in both worlds."

"How so?"

"I'm a quarterback coach during football season and fill in the rest of my hours with the company that Liz and I run with my sister. I never thought I'd go back to football. If I couldn't play, I wanted no part of it, but then I started to miss it, and my old coach hounded me to come back."

Michael's words resonated with Cole. While he didn't miss the pressures and long hours of his old career, he did miss the challenges and the satisfaction of accomplishment.

"Maggie is cool," Michael added, giving him a pointed look. "Just so you know, she has a lot of friends who look out for her, including me. She doesn't have family around, but she does have us, and I owe her a lot for everything she did to make the wedding perfect for Liz and myself."

He smiled. "I appreciate the warning. I like Maggie, but I'm leaving Napa in a week, so..."

"So don't hurt her on your way out."

"I won't," he promised, meeting Michael's gaze head on. At least he hoped he wouldn't.

Michael gave him a long look as if judging his sincerity, then said, "All right then. Let's buy some food."

"So, where did you find Cole?" Liz asked as Maggie sat down next to her.

"He found me," Maggie replied. "His aunt owns the Stratton. He came for a visit and we met."

"Wait! Is this the guy who kissed you out of the blue?" Julie interrupted, curiosity in her gaze.

"Yes, he was just being funny," she said. "It wasn't a big deal."

"But you're here with him now, so things didn't end after that kiss," Julie commented, a thoughtful gleam in her eyes.

"No, they didn't, because his aunt asked me to show him around Napa. We did a wine tour yesterday and when Julie mentioned she had an extra ticket for today, I decided to bring him. He's a big baseball fan."

"And he's hot," Liz said with a grin. "Glad to see you

aren't completely hibernating up in Napa."

"Napa is not the end of the world," she said defensively. "And my life is just fine, thank you. Just because you all have love fever doesn't mean I have to be on the hunt for a man every second of my life."

"Well, not every second," Liz conceded. "But once in a while… It's been years since you dated anyone for more than a few months."

"And Cole is not going to break my record," she said. "He's leaving town next week. So that will be that."

"Too bad," Jessica put in. "You two look good together."

"Looking good together doesn't mean we'd *be* good together," she said. "We have different goals. Cole is an adventurer. He wants to travel, see the world, and you all know that's the last thing I want to do."

"Maybe it would be different seeing the world with a man you care about than being forced to move around as a kid," Jessica suggested.

That thought had crossed her mind, but she wasn't going to say it out loud, because it would make Cole seem more important than he was. "Let's talk about you, Jess. Are you going to move back to the Bay Area?"

"I am," Jessica said with a happy light in her eyes. "In January. I just got hired for a teaching position in Half Moon Bay. It starts after the holidays, which will be perfect. I'll have enough time to pack up and move from San Diego. It will also be a better time for Brandon to switch schools. He's only in second grade, so I'm hoping the transition will be smooth." Her affectionate gaze settled on her son who was throwing a tennis ball up in the air and catching it with his oversized baseball mitt.

"He'll be at your school, so you can keep an eye on

him, right?" Julie asked.

"Yes, and we'll be close enough to my mom that I can check in on her more often. She's been battling some health problems, so I'll feel better being only fifteen minutes away. Plus, I'll get to see you guys. I miss you all so much. It's been hard to be so far away when all the fun is happening up here."

"We miss you, too," Maggie said. "It's not enough to just see you at our weddings, although those do seem to be happening fairly frequently. By the way, has anyone talked to Isabella recently? Has she set a date yet?"

Her friends shook their heads. "Maybe Kate knows," Jessica said, seeing the dark-haired blue-eyed Kate coming down the stairs.

"I made it," she said breathlessly. She gave everyone a hug, with Maggie coming up last. "Maggie, you came. I'm so happy."

"I said I was coming," she replied.

"I know but you've been bailing out of a lot of our group outings lately."

"I've been busy."

Kate dismissed that excuse with a wave of her hand. "We're all busy. You still have to put friends first."

"You guys are always first," she said.

"Or maybe second now," Liz said with a mischievous smile.

Maggie shot Liz a dark look.

Kate glanced from Liz to Maggie. "What did I miss?"

"Maggie brought a date, and he's very good-looking," Liz said.

"Really?" Kate said with a speculative gleam in her eyes.

"It's nothing. You guys always make a big deal out of

nothing."

"You know you can't bring a man around us without getting some questions," Kate said. "What's he like besides being attractive?"

"He's smart, very intuitive." She paused, thinking there were so many ways to describe Cole and yet none of the adjectives that came to mind did him justice. "I've had some of the best conversations with him. I feel like I know him better after a few days than I knew some of the guys I dated for months. But he's leaving in a week, so nothing is going to happen. I can't get involved with someone who doesn't live in Napa."

"Where does he live?" Julie asked.

"He's traveling at the moment, but I think he'd say Los Angeles is home."

"He's traveling?" Kate echoed. "Is he independently wealthy?"

"He had a big job for a long time. Now he's taking time off. I think he has some cash in the bank, but he doesn't wave it around. He's not like that."

"You like him," Julie said with a knowing nod.

"Really, really like him," Jessica put in with a smile. "And he's just your type. Longish hair, faded jeans, scruffy beard. Reminds me of the guys you dated in college."

"He does," Liz agreed. "I thought you said you were off bad boys."

"I am. And let's not talk about the horrible choices I made in college. Besides all that, did you all not hear me say that he's leaving soon?"

"Well, he's here now," Julie said. "It's so hard to find someone you really like. Do you want to dismiss him just because of geography?"

She stared at four of her closest friends in the world and knew they had her best interests at heart, but she also knew that Julie and Liz were crazy in love with their men, and Kate was crazy about love, spending her days as a wedding planner, which only left Jessica to understand. She turned to the woman who had once shared a dorm room with her. "You get it, Jess, don't you?"

"I do," Jessica said with a nod. "Long-distance relationships are difficult. Actually, most relationships are hard even under the best of circumstances. If he's leaving, then maybe you should be careful with your heart. We all know how big it is and how easily it can be broken."

"No risk, no reward," Liz cut in. "You can't run away from something just because it might not work out. That's not what life is about, Maggie."

Trust Liz to suggest she be a little more adventurous and daring. Liz had always been the one to encourage all of them to reach for the stars.

"But it's her life," Jessica argued. "Her decision."

"Thanks, Jess." She smiled at the rest of them. "I love all of you so much. And I do hear what you're saying. But I have a plan, and Cole doesn't fit into it."

"Well, you know what they say," Liz said dryly. "Life happens when you're making plans."

"Changing the subject," she said purposefully. "What can you tell us about Isabella's wedding plans, Kate? Have they set a date yet? Because the three of us haven't heard a thing."

"They were going to do Valentine's Day, but now they're thinking March. I did look at some bridesmaid dresses with Isabella last weekend, but it's getting more difficult to find a color and style that we haven't used yet. I don't know where we'll end up when we get to the last person in this group."

"That will probably be me," Maggie said. "You'll all end up in pink polka dots."

"I will be after you, Maggie," Jessica said. "I have my hands full with Brandon. I'm not looking for another male."

"That's usually when they come looking for you," Liz said.

"Look, there's Matt," Julie interrupted. They turned their attention to the field. Matt gave them a nod and a wave, his gaze lingering on Julie's face before he joined his team.

Maggie was touched that the love between Julie and Matt was so strong that it was palpable from yards away. She had to silently admit a yearning to feel that way about someone.

No sooner had that thought crossed her mind when Michael and Cole came down the stairs, their arms filled with boxes of food and cartons of drinks.

She moved down the row as Cole crossed in front of Liz to sit next to her.

"I think we got enough," he said, handing one of the boxes to Liz and another to Jessica. "Michael and I decided to get plenty for everyone."

"It looks like you did that. I want to introduce you to Kate."

Kate walked down the row in front of them and shook Cole's hand. "Nice to meet you, Cole."

"You, too. You're the wedding planner, right?"

"You've done your homework," Kate said approvingly.

Cole grinned. "I did. Maggie gave me a little prep in the car, but she didn't tell me how attractive her friends were. No wonder everyone is getting married. I don't know how you've all stayed single this long."

Kate laughed. "And you're a charmer."

"Just speaking the truth."

"That's enough, Cole," Michael put in. "You're going to make me look bad."

"No one could make you look bad, honey," Liz said, giving Michael a smacking kiss on the lips.

"Thanks, babe."

Maggie turned her attention toward the field as the announcer called for everyone to stand for the national anthem. She put the box of food on the seat while a singer from the San Francisco Opera gave an amazing rendition of the song.

Then it was time for the players to take the field.

As they sat back down, she said, "Today is going to be fun, Cole."

"Today became fun when you opened your front door this morning, Maggie."

"That's a nice thing to say."

"I mean it. As Michael said, 'you're something special.'"

"He told you that?"

"Right before he warned me not to mess with you, but he didn't have to tell me that, Maggie. I already knew you were special."

Their gazes clung together for a long moment, and then she drew in a deep breath and grabbed a garlic fry. She needed something to back Cole away and garlic was as good a weapon as any.

—————

Cole enjoyed the game, not just because he loved baseball, but also because it was fun to see Maggie with her friends. He liked the way Maggie, Liz and Kate supported Julie, who got nervous every time her fiancé stepped up to the plate. Not that Julie had anything to be worried about. Matt Kingsley started out with a triple, following it up with a double in the fourth inning. The man was definitely an all-star.

Cole also liked watching Michael and Liz together. Liz had a sharp, sarcastic wit, but Michael was a good match for her, and when they weren't challenging each other over something, they were laughing or exchanging a quick kiss. It was clear they were not only madly in love, they were also best friends.

And then there was Maggie. She was more fun than the rest of them put together. She cheered loudly for every hit and catch, getting nervous as the score bounced back and forth between the teams.

"I wish they'd go ahead by like five runs," she told him in the sixth inning. "Then I could relax."

"It's more exciting when it's even," he returned.

She clearly didn't agree with him. When they reached the ninth inning, the score was still tied. The first batter took a walk and the next two hitters struck out, which brought up Matt Kingsley with two outs in the bottom of the ninth and the winning run on first.

It wasn't just Maggie who was tense now; the entire stadium was energized, worried but also confident that the Cougars' hero could save the day one more time.

"He can't get out," Julie said tightly. "He has to move the base runner. He has to keep the game alive. He'll hate himself if he leaves the winning run at first."

"He can do it," Maggie said, putting her hand on

Julie's shoulder. "I have faith."

"Oh, man, I can't watch," Julie said, covering her eyes as Matt fouled off the first pitch for strike one.

"I can't watch, either," Maggie told Cole.

"I can tell you what happens."

"But I can't not watch, either," she said with a groan.

Matt fouled off a second pitch—strike two.

"It's still a tie game even if he gets out," he said. "We can't lose here; we can only win. You need to breathe."

"Well, I don't want to be tied. I want us to win," Maggie said.

"So do I," he replied. "I think he's going to get a hit."

"There's so much pressure. Why would anyone want to do this?" Maggie asked, as Matt took ball two.

"This is what ballplayers live for," he said. "Every kid who plays baseball in his backyard or at the local park dreams of being in this exact position: bottom of the ninth, two outs, playoff game on the line. It doesn't get better than this."

"He's right," Michael chimed in. "Except for me, it was fourth quarter, ten seconds on the clock, game on the line."

Cole nodded as Matt took ball three. "He could walk him. There's an open base."

"Mantilla has been hitting well, too, though," Michael interjected. "It would be a risky move."

"That's true."

Cole smiled at Maggie as she slid her hand into his. "He's got it. Don't worry."

"I hope you're right."

The pitcher wound up and then threw to the plate. With a swing and a powerful crack of the bat, the ball soared into the sky and over the right field fence into the bay. Cole had expected a hit, but a homerun was even better.

The crowd went wild. Maggie threw her arms around him, hugging him, then kissing him, then turning around to hug everyone else. There was pandemonium in the stadium as the winning run crossed home plate, and the team rushed the field to celebrate Matt's homerun.

Julie looked dazed but happy as she accepted congratulations. "I can't believe it," she said. "That was too close."

"Don't tell your fiancé that. Tell him you never had a doubt," Jessica advised.

"Matt knows what a nervous wreck I am at these games," Julie said with a laugh. "I'm just glad he pulled it out. And we get to do all this again tomorrow. You're all coming back, right?"

Cole wished he was coming back, but he doubted he was on the invitation list for a second game. Plus, he did have his aunt's business to take care of.

"I have to work," Maggie said.

"We'll miss you," Julie said. "Cole, you're welcome to come if you want."

"Thanks, that's very generous, but I need to spend some time with my aunt tomorrow. This was great. I really appreciate the ticket."

"Well, don't run off. We're all going out for dinner. You two are coming," Kate said firmly.

"Is that all right with you?" Maggie asked Cole.

"Sure." The last thing he wanted to do was end this amazing day with Maggie.

"It's early, so it won't be a late night." She started to pull her hand away from his, but he held on tight.

"I don't want to lose you," he said, meeting her gaze.

"I don't want to lose you, either," she replied.

She was just talking about getting lost in the crowd, he told himself. And that's all he was talking about, too, right?

Chapter Eleven

After a fun celebratory dinner, Maggie and Cole left the rest of the crowd to party while they headed back to Napa around eight. "Everyone really liked you," she told Cole as she drove home. "You fit right in."

"I liked them. You have a good group of friends, Maggie."

"I'm really lucky. We all have different personalities, but we seem to bring out the best in each other."

"I could see that. Kate is the romantic. Liz is the sarcastic, cynical one. Julie is quiet and thoughtful but with a fun side when she's not stressed out about Matt getting a hit."

"Three for three," she said with a laugh. "What about Jessica?"

"I didn't get as good of a read on her. She spectates a little. She stands apart sometimes. I don't know if that's because she's the only one who's divorced and has a child or if it's just her nature to be on the outside of the circle."

"She was never on the outside when we were in college," Maggie said, thinking about his comment. "But maybe she has been since then. I feel bad that I may have left her out unintentionally." She paused. "I think things will change when she moves back here in January. Then we'll get to spend more time together."

"You're pretty far away from the rest of the group."

"An hour and a half is not that distant."

"It is for drop-in evenings or spontaneous yoga classes."

She smiled. "Trust me, yoga would never be a spontaneous event for me."

"You know what I mean."

"I do. So you described everyone but me. How do you see me when it comes to the group?"

"You're...special."

"Okay, I'm not liking the word *special*, because it could mean I'm special like in howl-at-the-moon, talk-to-herself special."

He laughed. "You do talk to pumpkins but I haven't heard you howl at the moon yet."

"Come on, Cole, you have to give me more than special."

"You're a nurturer, Maggie. You're the one they want to tell all their problems to, the one they trust completely."

"Sometimes they treat me like the little sister," she commented. "It's not bad, and I'm technically the youngest by like two months, but they're always looking out for me, and sometimes I don't believe they think I make the best decisions."

"They might worry for you, but they know you can take care of yourself. You're soft when you need to be and strong when you need to be. It's one of the traits I like most about you. You're not all one thing."

His words touched her deeply. She'd never had anyone really see her for everything she was, not just what was obvious. She blinked away some moisture from her eyes and focused on the road. "That's enough about me."

"I'm not sure I can ever get enough," Cole said somewhat cryptically.

She wanted to ask him what he meant, but she was afraid she wouldn't get the answer she wanted. In the end, she turned on the car radio and filled the silence between them with music.

They got back to her house around nine thirty. Cole walked her to the front door.

"Thanks for inviting me, Maggie. I had a great time."

"Me, too." She clutched the keys to the house in her hand, knowing that she had a decision to make, and she had to make it now. "I can't ask you in. I want to, but I can't. It would be different if you lived here, if there was a possibility of something longer than a few days, but that's not the case."

His serious gaze met hers. "I know. It's not a good idea."

"I thought you'd put up more of a fight," she said, not sure how she felt about his easy agreement.

"You know what you want, Maggie, and I know what I want."

"And they don't match up." She sighed. "But we had fun."

"We did, and our time together is not completely over. I'll be around another week, and I would love to see how you're going to get that massive pumpkin to the judging table at the Harvest Festival."

"I haven't figured that out yet."

"I'm not surprised," he said, putting his hands on her waist. "You're a big planner in some ways but fairly unprepared in others."

"Part of what makes me *special*," she said with a laugh.

"This is the other part," he murmured, as he gave her a long, tender kiss.

The slam of a car door and footsteps coming down the sidewalk broke them apart.

Maggie was shocked to see her landlord, Antonio Pastorini, coming across the grass. Antonio was in his early seventies and had gray hair, dark eyes, and the olive skin of his Italian ancestors. He lived a half mile away, and she saw him fairly regularly as he liked to pick up his rent in person and check on the property. Sometimes, she thought his visits were just an opportunity for him to talk to someone. He was a lonely widower, having lost his wife two years earlier.

"Mr. Pastorini," she said. "Is something wrong?"

"I'm afraid so. I'm sorry to come by so late and to interrupt your evening, but something has come up, and I wanted to give you as much notice as I possibly could."

"All right." She looked at Cole. "This is Antonio Pastorini, my landlord. This is Cole Hastings."

"Hello," Cole said with a nod. He turned to Maggie. "Maybe I should head out."

"Please don't go. This won't take long," Antonio said. "I just came by to tell you that I've decided to move to Miami to live with my sister. I just can't take the quiet anymore. I'm talking to walls all day long. I'm old and I'm tired, and my life isn't here anymore. I've finally come to accept that."

"Okay," she said slowly, not quite sure where she fit into his plans, but she had a bad feeling she was about to find out.

"I'm sorry, Maggie," he said heavily.

"What are you sorry about?" She thought she already knew, but she was still hoping for a miracle.

"I need to sell the house right away. My sister found me a place in Miami, but I'll need the money from the sale of both this house and the one I'm living in to make the move work."

"But I need six more weeks," she said, her mind spinning at the thought of losing the house after so much planning and saving.

"I wish I could give you that, but I spoke to a realtor today. She has buyers who can give me cash tomorrow, and I have to make a decision on the place in Miami by the end of the week."

"We had a deal, Mr. Pastorini."

The older man gave her a pained look. "Perhaps you could borrow some money, and I could still sell the house to you. I can give you until Friday to decide."

"That's really fast."

"I hope you can work it out. And I'm sorry again. Truly. You're a nice girl. But you're young. There will be other houses for you. I know you'll be all right."

She had a feeling he was trying to make himself feel better.

"We'll talk soon," he added. "Excuse me again," he said to Cole. Then he walked away.

Maggie felt dizzy and weak. Cole put a hand on her shoulder. "Are you okay?"

"I don't think so," she admitted.

"Let's go inside."

She nodded, then opened the door and walked down the hall to the kitchen. They sat down on stools at the island. "I can't believe I'm going to lose the house."

"Do you have a written agreement, Maggie?"

She gave him a blank look. "What?"

"A contract. I'm wondering if he can just up and decide to sell the house with a few days' notice. Did you have an agreement between you?"

"It was verbal. We didn't have a time frame."

Cole frowned. "That will make it more difficult."

"Difficult to do what? I'm done. I can't raise the money that fast."

"Maybe you don't have to. You could consult a lawyer, have him find a way to stop your landlord from selling until you can work out the verbal agreement you had."

"A lawyer sounds like more money I don't have," she said heavily.

"Well, that's probably true."

She stood up and paced restlessly around the room. "What am I going to do?"

"Would your father help?"

She immediately shook her head, horrified at the idea of asking her father for anything, because she knew exactly what he would say. "That's a no. He believes his children should stand on their own feet, and my brothers don't have money to spare."

"Maybe I could lend you the money," he said slowly.

"We hardly know each other."

"I know you pretty well," he said, meeting her gaze. "I'd like to help you make your dream come true."

It was tempting to say yes, to let him solve her problems. She'd been standing on her own two feet for a long time, but she couldn't agree to his proposition. If she was going to buy a house, make a home for herself, it had to be on her. "Thank you. That's incredibly generous. But

I have to say no."

"Are you sure? I've made some good investments over the years. I could give you an interest-free loan or a low-interest loan. We could work something out, I'm sure."

"You'd be taking a risk."

"No, I wouldn't. I've made riskier investments. I'd bet on you in a heartbeat, Maggie."

Her heart swelled at his words. "That's a nice thing to say."

"I mean it. How much do you need to cover the gap?"

"It doesn't matter, Cole. I'm not going to take your money."

"Why not?"

"Because it's your money."

"I don't need it right now."

"I have to do this myself." She sat down, trying to think of some other way to solve her problem.

"Okay, fine. Tell me more about Mr. Pastorini. What's his story?"

"His wife died two years ago. Since then, he's been lonely and depressed. He owns a small condo nearby, but he couldn't bear to live here after she died, so he rented the house to me. A couple of his other friends have moved away or passed away this year, and he has threatened to move before, but he seems very serious now."

"It's a hot market. He wants to cash out."

"Yes, I'm sure that's part of it. I just don't know why he can't wait six more weeks. It's not that long."

"No, it's not. That's your answer."

She looked at him in confusion. "What's my answer?"

"Mr. Pastorini is lonely. If you can cheer him up, get him involved in something, maybe he could hang on for a few more months."

"But the place in Miami needs an answer. And his sister is there."

"I'm sure there are other places in Miami. And his sister has probably always been there, right? You need to find a reason for him to stay in Napa a little longer."

"I can't imagine what that reason would be."

"Do you know any of his friends? Are there any women he spends time with?"

"I don't know much about his personal life. We've had coffee together a few times, but mostly he just tells me about his wife. I don't think he knows what to do with himself without her."

"You need to find him a date." Cole suddenly smiled. "This is great."

"What's great?" she asked, seeing the gleam in his eyes.

"I've got the perfect solution to your problem." He laughed. "A taste of her own medicine. We're going to set Mr. Pastorini up with my aunt."

Her jaw dropped. "You're not serious."

"Oh, but I am. A little payback will be sweet."

"Your aunt is my boss. I can't get her involved in my problems. It's not right."

"She won't know anything about your problems. What's your work schedule tomorrow?"

"I'm on the early shift—seven a.m. to three p.m."

"Perfect. Tomorrow you're going to invite Mr. Pastorini to have dinner with you to talk about your situation. He's already feeling guilty, so I'm sure he'll say yes. And I'm going to invite Aunt Ida to the same restaurant. We'll decide to share a table. It's going to be perfect."

"But what if they don't hit it off?"

"We'll figure that out when we get to that point. At the very least, Mr. Pastorini gets a night out with people to talk to, which might also help him to change his mind about moving away so quickly."

His excitement was contagious and she felt a wave of optimism run through her. "It might work. Thank you, Cole. I am so relieved, I could kiss you."

He opened his arms wide. "Go with the feeling, honey. Live for the moment."

She laughed. "You're something else, you know that?"

"Show me."

She leaned forward and kissed his hot, sexy mouth, then she said teasingly, "If things work out with your aunt and my landlord, there's more where that came from."

"Ah, incentive," he said with a grin. "I like it."

She smiled back at him. "And now I'm going to say goodnight, and you're going home, because you're still leaving in a week."

"Anchovies, onions, peppers, mushrooms, the works," Antonio Pastorini declared, looking at the menu in front of him. "I love a good pizza. But nobody makes it like my Angela used to. She had magic fingers. She'd knead the dough for long minutes to get it just the right texture."

Maggie smiled as she set down her menu and looked at the older man across the table from her. So far, the plan she and Cole had concocted was working perfectly. She'd convinced Mr. Pastorini to have dinner with her on

Tuesday night. Now Cole just had to show up with his aunt. "You must have had a wonderful marriage," she said.

"We fought like two alley cats for thirty years. But the passion..." His eyes darkened. "Nothing like it." He turned his gaze on Maggie. "Don't settle for less. Pick a man who makes you nervous and excited every time you see him."

His words made her think of Cole. Since he'd arrived in Napa, she'd been able to think of little else besides him, and she had to admit every time she saw him, she felt a jolt of electricity. But tonight wasn't about her and Cole. This dinner was about convincing Mr. Pastorini to stay in Napa and let her pay off the down payment on the house.

"Getting married is the last thing on my mind these days," she said.

"Why? You're not getting any younger. In my day, girls were married before they turned twenty."

"You know yourself better when you're older, and you know what you want from someone else. You don't get carried away by raging hormones."

"A little raging is good for the soul, Maggie. It keeps the blood thin; it doesn't clot up on you."

"I doubt that a medical doctor would agree with you," she said with a laugh.

"Trust me, I know what I'm talking about. I saw the way that young man was looking at you last night and the way you were looking at him. I definitely interrupted something between you two."

"Cole is just a friend, and he's leaving town in a few days."

"Then you better stop him from going."

"I can't. He has his life, and I have mine. We're not

really that compatible."

"Compatible is not everything. Bacon and eggs are compatible, but they'll kill you. Take champagne and strawberries, two different things, and together they're perfection."

"You have a point."

"So, are you going to tell me your plan?" Antonio asked with an arch of his thick gray brow. "I assume you've come up with some creative way to buy the house."

"I'm still working on that. You know how much I love the place."

"I do know, and I wish I could just give you more time, but the days are so long. My friends have moved away. I'm old and tired. I might as well spend my last days on a beach, see some palm trees and some bikinis."

Maggie smiled. "If you can still appreciate a good bikini, I think you have some life left in you. Besides, Napa is your home. Do you really want to leave?"

"It's not the same since Angela died."

"Well, maybe we could make things better. I could help you find some hobbies or meet new people." She paused. "It's not just about the house; I'd like to see you happier. You've been very nice to me. You're a really good man."

He cleared his throat with a rough cough. "We better order, before I choke on all this sweet talk."

As Antonio finished speaking, the door opened, and Cole walked in with Ida Stratton on his arm.

Maggie was relieved and happy to see them both. They made quite a pair, with Cole in black jeans and a gray plaid shirt and Ida in black leggings and a teal sweater top that complemented the sparkle in her blue eyes and the glowing smile on her face.

Out of the corner of her eye, Maggie saw Mr. Pastorini stiffen and sit up straighter in his chair, suddenly gaining a few inches of height and confidence. But then he swung his head in her direction and said, "What are you up to?"

"I don't know what you're talking about." Maggie smiled back with as much innocence as she could muster. "What a coincidence. There's Cole." She waved, and Cole nodded, whispering something in his aunt's ear as they made their way across the room.

Antonio stood up as Cole and Ida walked over to the table. Maggie jumped to her feet as well, feeling more than a little nervous now that the setup was at hand.

"Hello, Maggie," Ida said with a charming smile. "I didn't expect to see you here tonight."

Maggie cleared her throat, prepared to offer some rational excuse, but she didn't have a chance, because Ida had already turned her attention to Antonio.

"I'm Ida Stratton," she said, holding out her hand.

Antonio gently squeezed her hand as he gazed into her eyes. Finally, he spoke in a gruff voice. "Antonio Pastorini. It's a pleasure to finally meet you."

"Finally?" Ida murmured, a questioning note in her voice.

"I have seen you several times at the theater with your friend Christina. She was also a good friend to my wife Angela."

"Of course," Ida said. "Now I know why your name is familiar."

"Why don't you join us?" Maggie suggested. "We have plenty of room."

"Is that all right with you, Cole?" Ida sent her nephew

a questioning look.

"It's great," he said.

As they sat down at the table—Ida next to Antonio and Cole next to Maggie—Ida gave Maggie an enquiring look. "How do you and Mr. Pastorini know each other?"

"He's my landlord," Maggie replied.

"Oh. You own the house that Maggie wants so badly." Ida nodded her head in understanding as she glanced at Antonio. "She talks about her house all the time. I almost think she likes it better than my hotel."

"They don't compare," Maggie said hastily. "The house is more of a cottage, but it really is lovely, and I know Mr. Pastorini had many happy years there, too."

"Yes, but I would have lived anywhere with Angela. My wife," he added to Ida. "She died two years ago, bless her soul."

"I lost my husband many more years ago, but I still have the memories. I thank God for those," Ida said in commiseration.

"Have you two ordered?" Cole interrupted.

"We were just about to," Maggie replied, almost sorry he had broken up the conversation, but they had plenty of time to push Ida and Antonio together, at least for the evening. "We were thinking of getting a large pizza with the works, including anchovies, which Mr. Pastorini loves."

"I love them, too," Ida said with delight. "In fact, I adore them, and I never get to eat pizza with anyone who likes them."

"Ah, a woman who understands food." Antonio shook his head in amazement. "You never married again?"

"No, I never found anyone else I could really talk to

or enjoy spending time with. I like to have fun, and somehow I keep meeting very serious men."

"I know what you mean." He nodded in understanding. "Single women of my generation seem more interested in playing bridge or watching television. Me—I'd rather go dancing or listen to some live music."

"I also love to dance. There's a line-dancing class at the rec center that has a lot of people our age in it. You should come some time."

Maggie was thrilled by Ida's invitation. Getting Mr. Pastorini to see there was more to Napa than boredom was exactly what she'd hoped to accomplish.

"I'm not very good at line dancing," Antonio said. "But I can do the salsa."

Ida laughed. "I bet you can."

"So…" Cole said, clearing his throat. "I'm going to order the pizza now. Shall I get some bottles of wine or a pitcher of beer?"

"Red wine would be good for me, honey," Ida said.

Antonio nodded. "For me as well."

Maggie smiled and said, "Why don't you get a bottle?"

"I'll be right back."

As Cole went up to the counter to place their order, Ida and Antonio started talking about the history of the restaurant and their younger days in Napa.

Maggie couldn't believe how well it was all going. Ida was charming, and Antonio was responsive. With Cole in line for pizza, she was starting to feel like a third wheel.

"I was a contractor. I could fix anything, build any house in the world," Antonio boasted in reply to Ida's question about what he did for a living. "Then I got old, and now everyone wants a young, strong man." He pointed to his thin arms. "I may not have the muscle, but I've got the brain," he added, pointing his finger to his head.

"Experience counts far more than muscle," Ida agreed. "In fact, I have a young man who is supposed to remodel my suite, but he can't seem to understand the way I want to do things. He keeps trying to change my mind."

"But the customer is always right," Antonio replied.

"My thoughts exactly," Ida said. "The thing I'm really concerned about is closet space, Antonio. You don't mind if I call you Antonio, do you?"

"Of course not."

"And please call me Ida. Now, what do you think of those new closet inserts, where everything just snaps into place?"

"I know they're popular, but in my opinion, it's better to customize. Then you get it exactly the way you want it."

"Maybe Mr. Pastorini could give you some suggestions," Maggie interjected.

"That's a wonderful idea. If you have the time, of course," Ida added.

Antonio straightened in his chair, confidence filling his body, making him look bigger and more impressive. "It would be a pleasure."

"But don't forget you're planning to move to Miami next week," Maggie said. "You won't have much time."

Antonio tipped his head. "Perhaps I can push it back a day or two for a lady as lovely as this."

Ida laughed. "Oh, you are a charmer. I really would love your help. It's so difficult to find a genuine craftsman these days." She paused, her gaze drifting over to the counter where Cole was still in line then back to Maggie and Antonio. "I know this is a lot to ask but I wonder—do you think you could look at my suite now? I hate to break up your evening with Maggie, but I need to get started on the remodel this week."

"Well," Antonio said uncertainly. "It would be rude of me to leave."

"It's fine," Maggie said quickly. "Although you should go after we have pizza."

"Or," Ida said, "I could treat you to dinner at the hotel. Pizza if you like, but I have a chef who makes the most wonderful lasagna you have ever tasted."

Antonio brightened. "Lasagna is my favorite. I would love to help you out."

"Then let's go."

Maggie's mouth dropped open as they stood up. "But, but—what about the pizza?" she asked, wondering even as she spoke why she was trying to stop them.

"You and Cole have it," Ida said. "My nephew will only be around for a few more days," she added to Antonio. "I'm sure these two young people don't need us around."

"I'm sure they don't," Antonio said with a laugh. "We'll talk again later in the week, Maggie. We'll see what other ideas you come up with."

"All right."

Cole returned to the table with four wine glasses and a bottle of wine and gave her a questioning look. "Where did everyone go?"

"To the Stratton. Your aunt asked Mr. Pastorini to look at her suite and tell her what to do with her closets, and he agreed. She's going to treat him to dinner afterward."

Cole sat down. "That's an interesting turn of events."

"Our plan worked," she agreed, although she still felt a little unsettled about how it had all gone down.

"I guess," he said thoughtfully.

"What do you mean?"

"I didn't tell my aunt that we were trying to fix her up, and I can't imagine that she had a closet emergency, so I'm guessing she decided to take Mr. Pastorini away so you and I could be alone together." He grinned. "She doesn't quit."

"She did say she thought we'd be happy to spend time together. So what do you want to do?"

"Drink wine and eat pizza," he said pouring her a glass. "At least Mr. Pastorini won't be lonely for a few hours."

"No. I thought he and your aunt really hit it off, too. She told him he should come to her line-dancing class."

"What did he say?"

"That he was better at salsa."

Cole laughed. "Maybe they have more in common than we thought."

"Maybe they do. It would be nice if they got together."

"And a relationship between them would be good for you, too."

"Yes, of course, but it might be even better for them. Wouldn't it be crazy if our little plan resulted in them falling in love and maybe even getting married?"

"Whoa, Maggie. They're just looking at closets. Don't get ahead of yourself."

"You're right, but I'm telling you I don't think either one of them moves slow when it comes to what they want."

"You might be right about that." He paused as the waiter brought their pizza over to the table.

As Maggie glanced down at the pizza, she realized one thing she'd forgotten to mention earlier. "Damn."

He laughed. "You hate anchovies, don't you?"

"Yes. I meant to say get half-and-half, but I forgot."

"And I thought since the three of you wanted them, I'd just suck it up." He got to his feet. "I'm going to order another pizza."

"Really?"

"Yes. I think we should both have what we want, don't you?"

She nodded, but she couldn't help thinking that was a loaded question. Was there really any way they could both get what they want?

On a pizza, maybe—but in life she wasn't so sure.

Chapter Twelve

—➤➤◀◀◀—

Wednesday morning Cole knocked on the door of his aunt's suite just after nine. He hadn't spoken to her since the night before, and he not only wanted to see how the evening had gone but also to discuss the books he'd gone through yesterday afternoon. He had only begun to tell her about what he'd found when she'd hijacked Antonio from the pizza parlor. While he wasn't in a hurry to leave Napa, he did want to get the job done that he'd come to do. He might live a gypsy life, but he still felt a responsibility to the family business, especially when they were paying him to do some actual work.

Ida threw open the door, giving him a startled smile. Her cheeks were pink, and her eyes were sparkling. "Cole, what are you doing here?"

"I came to talk to you," he said, his brows knitting together as he heard a male voice in the background. "Are you with someone?" He had a hard time keeping the shock out of his voice.

"Yes, they're looking at my bedroom."

"They?"

Ida stepped back and let him into her living room. "Antonio and Doug."

He raised an eyebrow. "Mr. Pastorini?"

"Yes. After looking at my situation last night, he agreed to come back this morning and speak to Doug, the contractor I've been working with. Antonio understands what I want and what I need far better than Doug does. He's of a different generation; we do not speak the same language."

"You and Antonio really hit it off."

"We did. He's a charming man. I'm so glad you introduced us."

"You didn't have to whisk him away before pizza, you know."

Ida smiled. "I thought you and Maggie could use some alone time. And it was a good decision because Antonio is just what I need."

"For more than your closet?" he couldn't help asking, thinking his aunt looked like a giddy young girl this morning.

She waved his words away. "Cole, really, I barely know the man."

"Exactly. You should be careful, Aunt Ida. You're a wealthy woman." He felt a little guilty that he'd thrown them together.

"And you think it's only my money that can attract a man?"

"Well, no, of course not."

"Good, because I know a fortune hunter when I see one and that is not Antonio. He's an old-fashioned gentleman, and it's nice to have someone my age to speak to."

"You should still be careful. Sometimes you trust people too easily."

"It's the only way I know how to be, honey. And

frankly, I don't feel like being careful anymore. I'm going to live for the moment, just like you. Speaking of fun, how was your night with Maggie?"

"It was good. She's great." He cleared his throat. "But I'm leaving in a few days; that hasn't changed."

"You like her, don't you?"

"It would be hard not to."

"That's why you're spending all your time with her instead of helping me with my business."

"Which is why I came to speak to you. Can you give me the keys to Harry's personal office? I know I missed out on the opportunity to get into his office on Monday, but I'd like to get in there tonight when he goes home for the day."

"Of course," she said, her smile dimming a little as she walked toward the desk. "But I can't imagine what you'll find in there."

"Maybe nothing, but I need to look. Perhaps tomorrow we can sit down and talk about everything. I did go over the books, and I have looked around the rest of the hotel. I have some thoughts on the fitness center and the concierge."

She frowned. "You're finding too many problems, aren't you?"

"Let's just say I have some ideas for improvement."

"I feel like I should already know what those are."

"Sometimes it helps to have an objective viewpoint. You live here. You care about your employees. I'm not emotionally attached to anyone or anything; you are. That's why I'm here." He saw the distress in her eyes and was sorry he'd put it there. "We're on the same team. You know that, don't you?"

"I do. I just feel a little guilty for letting things get

sloppy, but you're right, that's why you're here. But now I should get back to the bedroom. I have some men waiting for me there. Goodness, I haven't said that in a while," she added with a laugh.

He grinned at her mischievous smile. "Just remember what you always say to me."

"What's that, honey?"

"It's never too late to start over."

"I do say that, and it's very true. Every time I start thinking I might be so old I'll just have to run out the clock, something happens and I realize I'm not dead yet."

"Far from it."

"You can start over again, too, Cole."

"No need. I'm happy with my new reincarnation."

"I hope so, but sometimes I wonder." As she finished speaking, Antonio called her name. "We'll talk later. I have to go."

"Okay," he said, but as he left her suite he couldn't help wondering what she'd meant by her last comment. Why on earth would she think he wasn't happy? He had the life of freedom most people dreamed of. He just didn't have one special person in his life. But he'd done the serious relationship. He'd tried to be a good husband, and he'd failed. Why would he want to try that again?

Maggie's name ran around in his head. "Not for me," he muttered, wishing he felt happier about that decision. Maybe he needed to get out of Napa sooner rather than later.

Wednesday afternoon was busy for Maggie with a lot of new guests checking in for the Harvest Festival. As two o'clock neared, she grew impatient for the end of her day. She was going to the Napa Fairgrounds right after work to enter her pumpkin in the Harvest Festival Pumpkin Contest, and she was excited to see how Henry would measure up.

"Finally, it's slow," Karen said, walking over to Maggie. "I can't believe the lines we've had to deal with. The hotel is completely sold out for the next five nights. I don't remember when that last happened."

"I'm glad business is going so well, but it's been crazy today." She glanced over her shoulder at the closed doors leading into the back offices. Harry Stone had been in and out every other minute, micromanaging her job and in general making her life miserable. She could hardly believe he'd left them alone for five minutes.

"He went on a break," Karen said, reading her mind.

"Good. He's been on me all day."

"He's definitely not your biggest fan. You're too friendly for his taste."

"I thought that was part of the job."

"Not when he's watching. He's more impressed with speed."

"I suppose."

"He's more on edge because Mrs. Stratton has been taking interest in our bookings since she came back from Europe. She was asking him a lot of questions last week, and he didn't like being put on the spot, that's for sure."

"He got used to running this place without her oversight."

"He did." Karen looked around the lobby, then added, "I think he might be having personal or marital problems."

"Why would you say that?"

"He met with a divorce attorney last week. The man came to the front desk and left his card. Harry had just stepped out for a moment. When I gave him the card and told him the man was waiting for him in the bar, he turned white as a sheet."

"That's interesting."

"But probably not that surprising. I don't know could anyone stay married to him. He's so difficult."

"I agree."

"So, changing the subject—how did your pie turn out? You're taking it down to the festival this afternoon, aren't you?"

"Not the pie. It just didn't come together, but I am still entering my giant pumpkin. Hopefully, he'll bring me home a ribbon of some color."

"How big is the pumpkin now?"

"I'm pretty sure it weighs over a hundred pounds."

"How are you going to lift it into the car?"

"I'm still working on that. I'm hoping the neighbor's son will help me when he gets home from school. He has a truck."

"I wish you luck. So have you seen our hottest guest lately?"

She hadn't told Karen about any of her dates with Cole. While she didn't usually keep secrets from her friend, she hadn't wanted to answer questions about him, mostly because she knew Karen would tell her to go for it and not worry about the future, and she didn't need another voice urging her to do something she would probably regret. "I haven't seen him today," she said lightly.

"I saw him in the gym yesterday morning before I came on duty. He looked really good in workout clothes.

His body is ripped. Abs that should be on a magazine cover."

Since her fingers had gotten up close and personal with some of Cole's ripped muscles, she silently agreed.

"I wouldn't mind going for a ride with him," Karen said. "And I'm not talking about his motorcycle."

She forced a smile onto her face, trying to ignore the incredibly shocking wave of jealousy that Karen's joking words had sent racing through her body.

"What about you?" Karen asked.

"I'm not a big fan of motorcycles."

Karen gave her a pointed look. "You know what I mean."

"He's not my type."

"Sexy is not your type?"

"He's a guest. He's leaving in a few days."

"Sometimes that makes it easier and more fun. You don't have to worry about the long-term. You don't have to go down the pro and con list as to whether he'd make a good boyfriend or want a relationship. You just have a hell of a good time for as long as it lasts."

"I want more than that. I want someone who will stick around, someone solid and stable and—"

"Boring," Karen finished with a sigh. She suddenly straightened and tipped her head toward the lobby doors. "Speak of the devil."

Maggie turned her head to see Cole jogging into the hotel wearing shorts and a t-shirt, his muscles gleaming with a fine sheen of sweat from what had obviously been a good run.

He gave them both a smile as he passed. "Hello, ladies."

"Hello, Mr. Hastings," Karen said.

Maggie swallowed hard and managed to get out, "Hi" as Cole headed toward the elevators.

As soon as he disappeared around the corner, Karen burst out laughing, and said, "Yeah, you're not interested in him at all."

Thankfully, Maggie was saved from answering as a middle-aged couple stepped up to the counter to check in.

―➤➤◀◀―

Cole smiled to himself as he got into the elevator, happy he'd had a chance to connect with Maggie when she wasn't busy with a customer. He'd tried to avoid her when they were both in the hotel. She had a job to do, and so did he, although he wasn't working particularly hard at it.

When he visited one of the family hotels, usually his days were filled with analyzing the books and marketing data, talking to the personnel and to the guests, and generally reviewing everything that was happening at the hotel. He'd spend his nights writing up reports on the customer service in the restaurants, the speed and reliability of room service, the cleanliness of the fitness center, the inventory in the gift shop, and the friendliness of the staff to all guests, whether they looked important or not.

But on this trip, he'd barely dug into anything. He told himself that was partly Aunt Ida's fault. She was the one who had set him up with Maggie in the first place, and she was the one who had encouraged him to explore Napa. Even though she seemed to have legitimate concerns about the hotel operations, he had to wonder if part of the reason she'd suggested he come to the hotel was to set him up with Maggie.

He inserted his key into the door and headed straight for the shower. While he wasn't completely sure of his aunt's motives, he did want to do a good job for her. She was one of the nicest people in the family, and he didn't want to let her down.

As he stepped under the hot spray of water, his thoughts turned from his aunt back to Maggie. It had given him a lift to see her beautiful blue eyes turn on him as he came through the door. He'd seen desire even in that brief connection, the same desire he felt for her. Leaving her each day was getting more and more difficult, which meant he should really make more of an effort to avoid her outside of the hotel as well as inside.

Maggie was not for him. She was sweetness and light, optimism and hope, and he was jaded and cynical. She wanted a happily ever after, a home, a husband, kids, days of growing pumpkins and making pies and being part of a community. *Well, maybe not making pies*, he thought with a smile, *but certainly everything else*. And he didn't want any of that.

He should have walked away and stayed away after their first breakfast together. Instead, he'd spent way too much time getting to know a woman he couldn't have. He needed to get his job done and get the hell out of town before he did something stupid like fall in love.

But hitting the road and heading for some unknown destination didn't seem quite as appealing as it once had. That would change, he told himself forcefully. As soon as he left Napa, he'd go back to being the free spirit he'd become.

After he finished showering, he dressed and sat down at his computer. He spent the next hour going over the hotel accounting reports his aunt had sent him, this time line by line. A few items jumped out at him; one was an order for very expensive sheets. His gaze drifted over to his unmade bed. Were the sheets in this room lower quality simply because he'd been given one of the worst rooms in the hotel? Or did the orders on the books not match up with what was actually in the hotel? Frowning, he made a note to check out the inventory of linens.

Then he opened up the file from human resources and started reading through the personnel reports. The worst reviews all seemed to come from Harry Stone. Every other department had what anyone would expect to see—good, bad, and in between—critiques, but Stone's reviews on the front desk employees were particularly harsh.

He saved Maggie's file for last, feeling a little guilty for invading her privacy, which was another reason why he shouldn't have gotten involved with her. He couldn't afford to get squeamish about looking at every detail in the hotel, including the beautiful desk clerk who got him all wound up every time he saw her.

Maggie was definitely on Harry's bad list. Stone felt she was too slow at check-in and check-out. She didn't keep enough boundaries between herself and the guests. She stepped outside her job too often, interfering with other departments to satisfy a guest's needs when she should have passed the task along.

Stone's last report had come in on Saturday, the day after he'd arrived. Stone reported the story of Cole's impulsive kiss in a very negative way, insinuating that Maggie flirted with the guests, going so far as to kiss someone at the front desk. Stone felt that Maggie was not a suitable employee and that termination should be considered.

His stomach turned over as he realized he'd put Maggie's position in actual jeopardy and the last thing she needed right now was to lose her job. But he wouldn't let that happen. Ultimately, Aunt Ida could overrule any of Stone's decisions.

As he ran through Stone's notes on Maggie, he realized there was a common theme behind them. Stone didn't like Maggie because she was sticking her nose in business that was outside the scope of her job. Was Stone worried that Maggie might catch him doing something he shouldn't?

He needed to talk to Maggie about her manager, and he needed to do that outside of the hotel.

Which meant he needed to see her again.

Excuse or not, he was going to take it.

A little before three o'clock, Cole headed downstairs. Maggie wasn't at the front desk, and he frowned. He'd thought he'd catch her before she left for the day. He picked up his pace, and jogged down the hall toward the entrance to the employee parking lot. As he turned the corner, he ran right into someone coming from the opposite direction. He threw out his hands to steady the woman, realizing happily that it was Maggie.

"Sorry."

"What are you doing out here?" she asked in surprise.

"I was looking for you. I thought I might catch you in the parking lot."

"Okay, but can you let go of me? I don't need Mr. Stone thinking I'm hooking up with a guest the second I get off my shift."

Cole tried to step back but found his wrist was caught on her sweater. "I'd like to let go, but..."

Maggie followed his gaze to where the threads of her sweater were tangled around the knob of his watch. "Damn. This is my good sweater."

Cole used his free hand to work on the tangle, but when his fingers came into contact with the soft curve of her breast, his mind had trouble focusing on the task at hand.

"Did you get it?" Maggie asked.

He shook his head, his throat a little tight. He didn't want to free his hand. He wanted to wrap the other one around her and lose himself in her arms, in her body.

"Hurry up," she commanded with a hint of desperation in her voice. "Mr. Stone could come by at any second."

"You worry too much."

"I really don't, not when it comes to my boss."

Okay, she had a point. Hadn't he just read her personnel file?

"Cole, please. This isn't the time or the place," she said.

"I know, but—I'm stuck on you." He gave her a smile.

She fought her response, but reluctantly her lips curved upward. "That's not funny."

"It *is* a little funny."

"Let me do it." Maggie pushed his hand aside and tried to see the problem. With some deft maneuvering, she finally untangled them. "There. You're free."

"Yeah, I'm free." As Cole said the word, a surprising heaviness settled around his heart. Being free was all he'd wanted for the past few years, but now the word rang hollow. He shook that thought out of his head. "Are you headed home?"

"Yes, but only to pick up Henry. The judging starts tonight."

She walked toward the parking lot, and Cole fell into step with her. "How are you going to get the pumpkin into your car?"

"I'm hoping my neighbor's son will help. He's supposed to be home after school today, and he has a truck."

"Why don't I help you? I'd like to see how Henry measures up to the rest of the competition."

"Don't you think you should spend some time with your aunt?"

"She's busy this afternoon. She's spending time with Antonio," he added.

That got Maggie's attention. "I was wondering how last night went, but I didn't see her today to ask her."

"It went very well. I stopped by her suite early this morning, and he was there looking at her closets and talking to her contractor. She said they were going to look at some cabinetry this afternoon."

"That's great. If he stays busy, he won't have time to talk to realtors. I'll get another paycheck on Friday, so I only need one more month to make my down payment."

"I'm not sure my aunt can keep him busy for a month." He also wasn't sure Maggie would keep her job for a month if Harry Stone had his way, but he wasn't going to tell her that now.

"You never know. Your aunt can be quite charming. I just want him to see that he can still have a good life here in Napa even without his wife. And I'm not being completely selfish. He's told me before that he really doesn't want to go to Florida, that he hates the heat."

He smiled. "You don't have to rationalize it for me, Maggie. I get it. And I hope it works out for you."

"So do I."

He walked around her car as she unlocked the doors and slid into the passenger seat.

She glanced over at him as she started the car. "Every day I think I've seen the last of you, and then there you are."

"That day will come," he said lightly.

"I know, but I think it should come soon. I'm starting to like you a little too much, Cole."

He was both startled and impressed by her candor, but then Maggie wasn't one to play games. "I feel the same way."

"Does it scare you, too?"

"More than you might think."

"But we both know where we stand, so..."

"So let's go get Henry and see how he does. That's all we have to do today, Maggie. Anything else can wait."

Chapter Thirteen

Maggie's neighbor's son, Kevin, backed his truck into the driveway and then he and Cole managed to tie ropes around the giant pumpkin so they could transport him more easily into the back of the truck. Cole volunteered to ride in the back of the truck to watch over the pumpkin while Maggie followed in her car. When they got to the fairgrounds, Kevin and Cole managed to get the pumpkin, with the help of a dolly, into the judging area. Maggie thanked Kevin with a fifty-dollar bill and then walked around the judging area to see how Henry stacked up with the competition.

"He's not as big as some of the pumpkins," Cole commented.

"No, but he's more attractive. He has good round symmetry and his skin is free of gouges and deformation. He has nice color, too."

Cole laughed.

"What?" she asked.

"I just can't believe you're talking about a pumpkin's skin and symmetry."

She made a face at him. "Well, I'm sure every other grower here is making the same analysis."

"I'm sure you're right."

"I think Henry has a chance to win something. The super giant pumpkins in the next room get a cash prize, but I'm just hoping for a ribbon to wrap around him."

"Just like a woman to want to put a noose around a man's neck," Cole teased.

"Only you would see it as a noose. I look at it as a proud moment for both Henry and me."

"And then what happens? Does Henry's proud moment end with him being carved up for display and his insides made into a pumpkin pie?"

"Don't mention the word pie to me," she said with a laugh. "I would like to carve him up for Halloween, though. He'll look good on the lawn for all the kids."

"Will you dress up to hand out candy?"

"If I have Halloween off—definitely. Mr. Stone hasn't done the schedule for that weekend yet, and I doubt he'll do any favors for me."

"You told me about the woman and her dog, but does your manager have something else against you?"

She shrugged. "He thinks I meddle too much, and I ask too many questions. I think that means I'm invested in my job and trying to make sure everything is good for our guests."

"What do you think of him as a manager? Does he do a good job running the hotel?"

"I'm not that impressed." She paused with a frown. "Don't tell your aunt I said that. If it gets back to Mr. Stone, I'll be in more trouble."

"Whatever you say to me stays with me, Maggie. I found the man to be rude and condescending on first impression, and that impression hasn't improved much since then. I had a brief conversation with him yesterday when I asked for housekeeping to come to my room later in the day. He told me he'd have to see if that was possible, and I never heard from him again."

"He doesn't like it when anyone wants to upset the schedule in any way. But he definitely shouldn't have told you that, Cole. I'm sure if he knew you were Mrs. Stratton's nephew, he'd have a heart attack."

"That shouldn't matter. My stay at the hotel should be good whether or not I'm related to the owner."

She nodded in agreement. "Of course it should. I've dealt with guests who have been impossibly rude, who've damaged the room, who've harassed the staff, but I always try to be professional and hear their side of the story. Some guests are just terrible, and we hope to never see them again, but I'd say that's a very small percentage." She paused. "Karen told me that she thinks Mr. Stone might be having some marital problems. Apparently, he met with a divorce attorney last week. Maybe that's why he's been in such a bad mood lately."

"Have you met his wife?"

"Once at a holiday party. She wasn't very friendly to me, and she didn't seem too excited to be at the hotel with her husband, but they've been together at least ten years." She paused, seeing a judge step up to the microphone. "They're about to announce the winners. Wish me luck."

"Always," he said, slipping his hand into hers.

Maggie held her breath as the winners were called out starting in tenth place. When Henry's name wasn't called, she started to get worried. Had he not placed at all? But finally the fifth-place yellow ribbon was awarded to her pumpkin.

"Sorry it's not blue, babe," Cole said.

"It's fine. I like yellow." She tried not to be

disappointed. It wasn't like growing a big pumpkin was a dream she'd had all of her life, but she had spent a lot of time nurturing Henry to get him where he was today.

"I don't believe you're fine." Cole gave her a thoughtful look. "What's that pumpkin really about, Maggie?"

"I guess it's a little about my mom, too."

"She grew giant pumpkins in addition to making apple pies?"

"No, but she was just so good at stuff like this. I know we talked before about me being me and not trying to be her. I just have to find a way to do that."

"You will. From what you've told me, it doesn't sound like you had a lot of time to sort through your grief and your anger. After your mom died, you were off to college, and your family was separated. You had to deal with a lot of emotions all by yourself."

"I didn't deal with them then."

"Which is why you're dealing with them now. It's a good thing, babe. You have to pull things out of hiding so you can look at them and get rid of them. Say good-bye to all the bad stuff. Let it go."

He was absolutely right. She hadn't realized how much of what she'd been focused on the last year had been about her mom, about her grief, her feeling of abandonment. She couldn't get her mom back, but she could make a life for herself that her mother would be proud of and that life really didn't need to involve pumpkins or pies.

She pulled her hand out of Cole's so she could put her arms around his neck and thank him with a kiss. "You're amazing. You probably just saved me thousands of dollars in therapy and pumpkin seeds."

He smiled. "Glad I could help."

"How did you get to be so insightful?"

"I made a hell of a lot of mistakes in my own life. I'm trying to learn from them."

"What kind of mistakes?"

"It's possible I've tried to avoid looking at myself by looking at other things."

"Like the open road?" she suggested, a gleam in her blue eyes.

"Exactly. Moving forward is all that matters. I don't really need a rearview mirror because I don't look behind me."

She stared back at him, realizing a sad fact. "I guess I'll be forgotten pretty soon then."

He didn't like her comment. "I didn't mean it that way, Maggie. I don't think I'll be forgetting you anytime soon." He paused and said, "So what do you want to do now?"

"I guess we should check out the rest of the festival."

"Sounds good." He took her hand in his. "Let's go have some fun."

She squeezed his hand and smiled in agreement. The clock was ticking down on their time together, and she was going to enjoy the last few minutes or hours or days—whatever they had left.

They spent the next two hours wandering around the fairgrounds, checking out harvest decorations, tasting wine, sampling fall treats, and listening to a soulful folk singer pour her heart out with her guitar and her voice. *Cole was the perfect partner,* Maggie thought. He was willing to try anything, and they found the same things either funny or amazing. They would often look at something and burst into laughter or send each other a questioning look. They were in perfect sync…for now.

But not forever, she reminded herself. She couldn't let herself fall in love with him, even though the butterflies flitting through her stomach told her she was already more than halfway there. Maybe Cole was right, though. The present was what mattered most. She'd put off whatever bad feelings might be heading her way until she had to deal with them.

They ate dinner at the festival, a delicious feast of butternut squash ravioli, salad, and pumpkin pie for dessert.

"Just think, this could be someone's Henry," Cole said, holding up his piece of pie. "Aren't you going to feel guilty eating it?"

"I have a rule. If I don't see the face, I can eat it."

He grinned. "I guess you've never gone fishing and cooked your catch."

"Nope," she said, taking a bite of pie. The cinnamon and ginger flavors were amazing. "I like pumpkin so much better than apple. I should have tried to make this pie instead."

He groaned. "Uh-oh. I feel another manic pie baking episode coming on."

She laughed. "I am not that bad, nor am I really that much of a homemaker. You've caught me in the middle of my nest-building phase. Before I moved to Napa, it was pretty much order-out, and I hadn't put my hands in dirt since I was twelve years old."

"It's good to make changes in your life. You don't regret what you try. You only regret what you don't try.

Someone wise said that—I can't remember who."

"At least you don't try to take credit for all your brilliant insights."

"Not unless it's due."

She finished her pie and said, "I think I need to walk off all the food we've eaten."

"I'm with you. We'll check out the booths we missed earlier on our way to the parking lot."

As she paused to check out an oil painting at one of the art booths, she suddenly saw a familiar face at the adjacent booth. As the man turned toward her, she pulled Cole around the corner of the booth, behind a large easel that blocked them from view.

"What's going on?" he asked in surprise. "Do you want to make out with me that bad?"

She frowned. "No, that's not what this is about. My boss is here."

"Harry Stone? Where?"

"Over there," she said, moving slightly to the right so he could see the booth next to them. Harry wore his usual navy blue suit, but he looked nothing like the rigid figure that hovered behind her in disapproval all day long. His tie hung loose around his neck, and he was talking with animation to a blonde woman, who appeared to be in her mid-thirties.

"Who's he with?" Cole asked.

"I have no idea. Oh, my God," she added when Harry put his arm around the woman and gave her a passionate kiss on the lips.

"I take it that's not his wife."

"Definitely not his wife. That woman is also a lot younger than him." She glanced at Cole. "I wonder if his wife knows."

"You said a divorce attorney came to the hotel, so I'm betting yes."

When she looked back at her boss, she saw him turn in her direction. "They're coming this way. I can't let him see me with you," she said, suddenly panicked that she'd trapped them between two booths and there was nowhere to hide.

"Why would he care?"

"Because you're a guest at the hotel. It's forbidden. I can't lose my job, Cole."

"I get it. I can solve this problem, Maggie."

Before she could ask how, he turned her around so his body was blocking hers and pulled her up against his chest in a passionate kiss.

Her heart pounded against her chest, both from the idea of being discovered by her boss and also the heat and intensity of Cole's mouth. Every kiss with him was different and better than the last. There were more nuances now, more time added in to explore, more emotion behind the physical attraction.

Cole lifted his gaze, gazing down at her with serious brown eyes, no trace of his usual lighthearted humor. "Maggie."

She had no idea what he meant by saying her name in just that way, but she did know that it had given her chills.

She drew in a breath and let it out, trying to remember where they were and what they were doing. Her boss... She looked around and saw no sign of Harry Stone. "I think he's gone. We should go. I don't want to risk running into him again, not with you. Sorry."

"I understand," he said quietly, emotions in his gaze that she couldn't begin to decipher. "Let's go."

They walked back to the car without running into

anyone else they knew. Since Maggie had driven Cole from the hotel, she took him back to the Stratton. She deliberately pulled into the farthest corner of the guest parking lot, not wanting to give the valet attendants at the front entrance anything to gossip about. "Do you mind walking from here?"

"No."

"Thanks for your help today, Cole."

"I'm glad I could get Henry to the festival for you. Are you going to miss him?"

She wasn't going to miss her pumpkin, but she was already missing Cole, and he wasn't even gone yet. "I'll survive," she said lightly.

Cole hesitated, and for a moment she thought he would kiss her again. But in the end he just said, "Goodnight, Maggie."

"Goodnight." She let out a sigh as he got out of the car and closed the door. If it was this hard to say goodnight, how difficult was it going to be to say goodbye?

Thursday morning, Maggie spent some time digging out the rest of her small pumpkin patch. She had six other pumpkins in the garden that she planned to give to the neighbors. The three houses closest to her all had little kids, so they would probably enjoy having extra pumpkins to carve.

As she set the pumpkins on the porch, a car turned in to her driveway. When Mr. Pastorini stepped out, her stomach clenched. She'd been hoping that not seeing him or hearing from him was a good thing, and that it meant he was too busy to be lonely or to be talking to realtors about selling her house. However, if he was still intent on moving to Miami before she had the money for the down payment, she was in big trouble.

"Hello, Mr. Pastorini," she said, as he walked across the grass.

His usually somber expression was gone. He had a smile on his face, a twinkle in his eyes. He didn't look like a weary old man anymore but someone young and alive and energized.

"Oh, Maggie, I am so happy," he said, putting his hand to his heart. "Such joy I haven't known in years."

"Because you're moving?" she asked tentatively.

"Moving? No. I'm not going anywhere. I've found the perfect woman. And I have you to thank for it. Ida has set my soul on fire."

Maggie couldn't believe what she was hearing or the transformation in the man who had seemed so despondent two days ago. "I'm so happy for you."

"And for yourself, no?" He laughed and shook a finger at her. "I'm not so old I can't see a setup. You wanted me to meet her."

"I did want you to see that staying in Napa had possibilities that you might not have considered, that there were people here you might not have met yet."

"The possibilities are quite attractive."

"Does this mean I still have a few months to complete my payments?"

"Take as long as you need. I'm not going anywhere."

She let out a sigh of relief, feeling an enormous weight slip off her shoulders. "You don't know how happy I am to hear you say that."

"It doesn't matter where I live as long as I have

someone to share my life with," he said. "Time passes so quickly, Maggie. You can't waste a single second. I know you're young and you think you have forever, but you'll be surprised how quickly the years can pass. Now, I have to go. Ida and I are going to meet with her contractor before lunch, but I wanted to let you know that the house will be yours as soon as you can make the down payment. I have the paperwork ready to go."

"I just need thirty more days."

"You've got them."

"I'll take good care of this house," she promised.

"I know you will."

"Thank you so much, Mr. Pastorini."

"You're more than welcome."

As Antonio left, she pulled out her phone and called the hotel switchboard, because she didn't have Cole's personal number. His deep, husky voice came across the line a moment later.

"Hello?"

"It's Maggie," she said. "I have some amazing news."

"I think I know what you're going to say—Antonio is in love with my aunt."

"You heard?"

"I just had breakfast with my aunt. She's over the moon about him. I couldn't believe it."

"He's just as madly in love with her. You made a good match, Cole."

He laughed. "Apparently. So you don't have to move?"

"No. Mr. Pastorini was just here. He's going to give me all the time I need to make the down payment. It's a miracle."

"I wouldn't go that far, but I'm really happy for you,

Maggie. I know you want that house more than anything else in the world."

"I do, and I owe it to you. It was your idea to bring your aunt to dinner."

"I'm glad I could help you out, although a part of me wonders if I didn't just help you chain yourself to a huge weight."

"You didn't."

"Well, you know what you want. Are you working today?"

"Yes, I'll be in at three."

"Maybe I'll see you."

"You know where to find me." She paused, feeling like there was more she wanted to say, but she couldn't find the words, so she quickly said, "Bye," and ended the call.

Chapter Fourteen

Cole approached the hotel front desk just as Maggie was about to take her dinner break at six. She gave him a smile, not letting on that she'd been watching for him all day. Now that he was here, her stomach was doing somersaults and her palms were sweating, and the man had done nothing more than say hello. But her body still remembered all the delicious, spine-tingling sensations of every intimate encounter they'd shared since he'd arrived.

"Break time?" he asked.

"How did you know?"

"My aunt told me you take a dinner break at six."

"Your aunt is always helpful," she said dryly, secretly pleased he'd made the effort to come by at her break time.

"I need your help," he said.

"One second." She grabbed her purse out of a drawer, told the other desk clerk she'd be back in an hour and then walked around the counter. "What do you need?"

He leaned forward to whisper in her ear. "I need you to get me between the sheets."

Her jaw dropped, and her head flew around to make sure that no one else had heard him. "Cole," she warned. "This isn't the place."

He laughed as he pulled back with a smile. "Relax. Your manager is in a meeting with my aunt."

"Still…"

"I actually meant that more literally than you might think."

She gave him a confused look. "Okay, you need to explain."

"Let's walk," he said.

"What are you up to, Cole?" she asked as they walked down the hallway.

"I want you to show me the hotel laundry, where the sheets and guest amenities are kept."

She stopped walking. "I can't do that."

"Why not?"

"Because you're a guest."

"I'm the owner's nephew."

"Then she can show you the laundry. Although, why you want to see it is a mystery to me."

"She can't show me; she's tied up with Mr. Stone, and I don't have a lot of time. I need someone like you to get me past the laundry attendants."

"Someone like me? Cole, what's going on?"

"My aunt has some concerns about the inventory. She asked me to take a look at the linens while she was speaking with Harry."

"What kind of concerns?"

"Can we talk about this in the laundry area? My request comes with my aunt's blessing. You won't get into trouble."

She gazed at him uncertainly. There was more to the story than he was saying, but he was Ida's nephew, and she'd obviously told him to find her, so…what could she do but say yes?

"Fine." She walked over to the elevator bank and pushed the down button. Once they reached the basement, she led him down another hallway to the laundry department. She said hello to Marti who ran the laundry and said she was checking on inventory for Mr. Stone, then she took Cole down another hallway and into an eight by ten foot room that contained the hotel linens and guest amenities.

She shut the door and faced Cole with her arms crossed in front of her. "Okay, talk."

"My aunt is worried that the hotel orders aren't matching up to the supplies. She thinks someone might be adjusting the books, and she asked me to take a look at the inventory."

"Why you?" she asked, having a sinking feeling in the pit of her stomach. "You didn't come here just to visit your aunt, did you?"

"Not completely. I came here to advise her on some business issues."

"And here I thought you didn't do business anymore."

"I occasionally consult," he admitted.

She wondered what occasionally meant, but Cole was headed to the shelves. He ran his fingers down a stack of sheets, digging around for a tag.

"When you said you wanted me to get you between the sheets, I didn't think you meant it literally," she commented.

He flung her a smile. "I wanted to get your attention."

"You really don't seem to have any trouble doing that."

"It works both ways, Maggie." He glanced back at the sheets. "These are not the high quality linens that were ordered. Would they be kept anywhere else?"

"No, this is it."

He moved over to another wall of shelves where the shampoos, soaps, and other guest items were kept. "This isn't the same shampoo on the order form, either. Damn."

"What does this mean?"

"Someone is padding the books. And I think it's your boss."

"Mr. Stone?" she asked in shock. "But he's so straight-laced, so self-righteous. I can't imagine he would do something dishonest."

"We saw him last night at the festival with a woman who isn't his wife," he reminded her. "You may not know Mr. Stone as well as you think you do."

She frowned. He had a point. "You're right. I don't actually know Mr. Stone, but still I'm surprised." She paused, drawing his gaze to hers. "Is it a lot of money, Cole?"

"Yes."

"What happens next?"

"I'll talk to my aunt. There are some other areas of the hotel that need to be investigated as well. We don't want Stone to know he's been made until we make sure we have enough evidence. You can't tell anyone about this, Maggie. We don't know if Stone is working alone or if someone else at the hotel is helping him."

"But I work here. You're asking me to keep things from my boss."

"Just for a little while. I know you want the best for the hotel, and you can't feel a lot of loyalty to Stone."

"I do love the hotel," she admitted. "All right. I'll keep quiet, but don't involve me in anything else."

"I won't."

She looked around the room. "Two guests

complained to me about the sheets last week. They said they were threadbare, and they were surprised at the quality. I reported their complaints to Mr. Stone, but he never got back to me. I asked him at the time if he wanted me to check with someone in laundry, but he told me to get back to doing my own job. Now, it's making more sense." Although, she still had trouble believing that her boss could be fixing the books. Then again, his behavior had changed while Mrs. Stratton was traveling. "We should go if you don't want anyone to get suspicious of what we're doing here."

Cole nodded and reached for the door. He turned the knob, then frowned, and tried again. "It's locked."

"What? I just pulled it shut."

"Apparently, it automatically locks."

"Let me try."

"Have at it."

She tried the door and had no better success. "I'll call Marti and get her to unlock the door." She pulled out her phone and connected with the hotel switchboard, but when they rang through to the laundry, there was no answer. "She's not picking up. I can't believe we're locked in."

"I doubt it will be forever," he said with a shrug.

"You really don't get bothered by anything, do you?"

"Well, not by this." He put his hands on her waist and pulled her close. "I know a great way to pass the time."

"You have a one-track mind, Cole."

He smiled. "And you're on that track, babe."

How could she resist an irresistible man? "You are so bad for me."

"Sometimes bad can be really, really good," he murmured against her mouth.

He was right again. Wrapping her arms around his back, she took his kiss and made it her own as passion quickly ignited between them. He undid the top three buttons of her white blouse, sliding his fingers under the strap of her bra, then delving lower to cup and caress her breast.

"You're driving me crazy," she muttered, as he kissed the side of her neck and slid his mouth down to her collarbone. "Don't stop," she breathed.

"I don't want to."

But even as he said the words, Maggie heard a rumbling at the door, voices that slowly slipped into her consciousness. "Oh, God, someone's coming in!" She jerked away from him, her hands rushing to the open buttons on her blouse. She wasn't fast enough.

The door opened, and Mr. Stone walked in, anger in his eyes. "What are you doing in here, or do I need to ask?"

"We got locked in," Maggie explained quickly.

"Get out, Miss Gordon, and I mean out," Harry said. "Out of the closet. Out of the hotel and out of my life. You're a disgrace to your uniform and to the Stratton. You're fired."

Maggie stared at him in shock as she finally managed to button up her blouse.

Cole put a reassuring hand on her shoulder. "Hold on there," he said. "This is my fault."

"No, this is none of your business," Mr. Stone interrupted. "Guests are not permitted down here. This is employees only. If Miss Gordon brought you down here, that's on her."

Obviously, Harry still didn't know that Cole was Ida's nephew, Maggie realized.

"Your final paycheck will be mailed to you, Miss Gordon."

"Please, wait, I can explain," she said, but her manager had already left the room and was quickly walking down the hall. "Dammit," she said to Cole. "What am I going to do now? Why didn't you tell him who you were?"

"I couldn't do that, Maggie, not yet. But I'll get you your job back. You don't have to worry."

She wanted to believe him, but she had no idea if he had the power to do that or how long it would take. "That's easy for you to say. But you might have just cost me my house."

He frowned. "It always comes back to the house, doesn't it?"

"Why shouldn't it? It's my dream. It might not matter to you, but it's everything to me."

"Mr. Pastorini said he would give you the time you need."

"That was today. Who knows how he'll feel tomorrow. I won't rest until I see my name on the deed."

"That will happen. This is just a blip."

"Maybe to you, but I never should have agreed to help you spy on my boss. I was an idiot. And now look where I am. You need to leave, Cole. You're the wanderer, so why don't you go wander somewhere else and leave me alone?"

She stormed out of the room, heading straight to the parking lot. She wanted to get into her car before the dam of tears burst. She couldn't believe she'd just gotten fired. When would she learn to mind her own business and not try to help other people? It so often backfired on her.

Cole had told her not to worry, that he would fix

things with his aunt. She certainly hoped that was the case, but at the moment her only reality was that she was now out of a job.

She'd thought she'd solved her housing problems when Antonio had fallen for Ida, but it looked like she wasn't out of the woods yet.

———

Cole entered his aunt's suite feeling pissed off and guilty for getting Maggie fired. He would get her job back for her—he had no doubt about that—but he had certainly complicated her life.

"I thought you were going to keep Mr. Stone here for an hour," he said when his aunt opened the door.

"I tried. He got a text and said he had to leave. I could hardly stand in front of the door. What happened?"

"I asked Maggie to help me get into the laundry room. We accidentally got locked in, and when the door opened, Harry Stone was there. He fired Maggie on the spot."

"For taking you into the laundry?"

He cleared his throat. "We might have been fooling around a little too."

"You were having sex in the laundry room?"

"No," he said emphatically. "We were just kissing." He saw the light of amusement enter his aunt's eyes. "It's not funny. Maggie got fired."

"Well, that's just ridiculous."

"Not according to Stone. He said she was a disgrace to her job and the hotel."

"Where is she now?"

"Probably at home. She ran out of the hotel pretty fast."

"We'll make it right, Cole. Tell me—what did you find?"

"Exactly what I thought: cheap sheets and generic amenities, nothing like what was allegedly ordered. I'm confident he's the one cooking the books. In fact, I think someone texted him because we were in the laundry room and his crimes were about to be exposed. It's time to confront him."

"It's still so difficult to believe he'd steal from the hotel, from me. I trusted him while I was gone. I gave him a raise, because I thought I could count on him."

"Maybe things changed when his marriage began to crumble and he got a young girlfriend. He probably needed more cash. Who knows? The reason doesn't matter. He needs to go."

"You're right. This is my fault, Cole. I got tired of running the hotel and ran off to see the world and let the business decline. I've let the family down."

"You can salvage the business. You've caught Harry before he can do real damage."

"I hope so."

"If you're tired of running the hotel, why don't you give it up? I'm sure the family could put someone else at the helm."

"I hate to be a quitter. And I do love the Stratton. I like living here, and I'll like it even more once my bedroom is redone. I enjoy the guests and the events and meeting new people. I just don't know that I want to be super involved in the daily operational details. I thought I could trust Harry, but that was a mistake."

"I'm sure you could find another manager. But you need to do what makes you happy. If it's this hotel, great. If it's not, then do something else. Life is short."

She smiled. "I think I was the one who first said that to you."

"When Carole and I split. You were right then, and I'm right now. I don't want you to feel trapped in your life. I know what that feels like. It's not good."

"I don't want to feel trapped, either, especially now that Antonio and I have met. I know it's only been a couple of days, but sometimes you don't need any more time than that."

Her words hit close to home. Maggie felt right to him, but he didn't want a relationship, particularly not with a woman who wanted a home and roots and all the things that had trapped him before. He wanted to be free to roam, to do whatever he wanted.

"What do you think I should do now?" Ida asked, drawing his attention back to the matter at hand.

"Call our attorney and fill him in, so we make sure we follow the proper steps to terminate Mr. Stone's employment. We also need to get a forensic accountant to go through the books in great detail. It's possible the hotel accountant was working with Harry. We need to know if anyone else is involved in skimming money from the hotel."

She sighed. "Such nasty business."

"If you want me to make the calls with you, I will."

"I would like that, Cole."

"We can do it in the morning."

"I'll call the attorney now. He's a friend. He'll pick up."

"Great. The sooner the better."

She nodded as she reached for her phone on the side table. "You know, Cole, I might need an interim manager at the hotel until I can replace Harry. You would be perfect for the job."

"I don't run hotels, Aunt Ida."

"You could run any business, Cole—you know that."

"I don't want to run a business. I don't do that anymore."

"This would only be temporary. It would give you more time with Maggie."

As much as he wanted more time with Maggie, it would be better to cut the ties now before he fell in love with a woman who felt right but was absolutely wrong for him.

⸺⸙⸙⸺

Friday, around noon, Maggie was on her knees, digging in her garden, taking out her frustration on a pile of weeds. Cole had called her the night before to tell her to hang tight and not panic, that he would fix everything. She hoped that was true. She really wanted to get her job back. But she'd hoped she would have heard something before now.

She looked up as the roar of a motorcycle came down the street. Cole turned into her driveway and got off his bike. She stood up, as he took off his helmet and walked toward her. She wondered if there would ever be a time when she didn't get goose bumps at his arrival.

She pulled off her gardening gloves. "I hope you have good news for me."

"I do," he said with a smile. "You better get cleaned up. You're back to work today at three."

Relief ran through her. "What about Mr. Stone?"

"He's been terminated."

"Really?" She was shocked it had happened that fast.

"Yes. He's been skimming money from the hotel for at least a year. My aunt and I confronted him, along with the hotel lawyer, this morning and he broke down and admitted what he'd done."

"I'm surprised he would admit it."

"My aunt got it out of him. She was both charming and forceful. I was impressed." He paused. "I'm sorry you got caught in the middle, Maggie. I wish I could have been completely honest with you, but my aunt asked for confidentiality. She'd seen some anomalies in the books, and she needed an objective opinion. I've done the same thing at a couple of other family hotels, not because of theft but because of inefficiency or a drop in bookings."

"So you're not *just* a gypsy?"

"Mostly I am, but occasionally I pick up a job here and there to help out the family."

That made sense. She'd always felt that Cole was holding something back; now she knew what it was. She wished he would have told her earlier, but she could understand why he hadn't. She licked her lips as she forced herself to ask an important question. "Now that you've figured out the problem, are you leaving?"

He slowly nodded. "Later today."

Her heart sank. "That's fast."

His lips tightened. "I think it's best. A few more hours would only make our good-bye harder."

She was disappointed that they had to say goodbye at all, but there was nothing she could do about it. He'd never lied to her about who he was and what he wanted in life. She couldn't do anything but wish him well. "Where will you go next?"

"I'll probably drive up the coast to Mendocino and spend some time on the water."

"That sounds nice." She drew in a deep breath and stuck out her hand. "Good-bye, Cole."

He ignored her hand and leaned over to kiss her. She soaked up every bit of that kiss, knowing it was the last one. When they pulled apart, she felt incredibly sad and had to fight back the tears. She wasn't going to cry in front of him. "Safe travels."

"Thanks," he said, dark shadows in his eyes. "Maggie, if I'd met you at a different time…"

"I know. I get it. I want you to be happy, Cole. You deserve it."

"So do you. I hope all your dreams come true."

"Yours, too. I better get dressed for work." She ran into the house as the first tear slipped out of her eye.

She shut the front door behind her and leaned against it. She wanted to hear the roar of his engine so that she would know he was gone. But she also wanted to hear his footsteps on the porch, hopelessly wishing one last time that he'd say he'd changed his mind and would stay with her forever.

Her tension increased with every quiet second, and then she heard the rev of the motorcycle engine. It was loud and then faded away. Cole was gone.

It was okay, she told herself determinedly. She had her job back and she would get her house. Her life was going to go exactly according to her plan. She would forget Cole. He would be just a good memory one day, wouldn't he?

Chapter Fifteen

——➤➤◀◀◀←——

Five weeks later, Maggie started her Friday morning shift at seven with a sad pit in her stomach. She missed Cole. Since he'd left, she hadn't been able to escape the deep feelings of loss and regret, which she tried to tell herself was silly. She'd known him a week. He shouldn't still feel so important to her, but somehow he did.

She thought about him every night when she went to bed and every morning when she got up. Every time she saw a motorcycle, she expected to see his sexy grin, his dark brown eyes, and his tight jeans. But it was never him; it was always someone else.

She looked up as Karen came out of the office.

"Here's your paycheck," Karen said, handing her an envelope. "This is the one, right? The one that puts you over the top?"

"It is." She took her check, feeling a wave of emotion. She finally had her down payment. As soon as she handed the money to Antonio, she would initiate the official purchase of her home. It would finally be hers. She wouldn't have to move ever again.

"You don't look as happy as I thought you would." Karen gave her a quizzical look. "But then you haven't looked happy in a while, which doesn't make sense, because so much around here has changed for the better with Mr. Stone out. We have a new manager who is very positive and supportive. Business is booming, and you're about to get the house you've been working toward for so long. So what's going on, Maggie? Is it Cole's absence that's putting those lines around your eyes?"

She hadn't shared much about Cole with Karen, but her friend was smart enough to know that something had happened between them, especially after Marti had spread their laundry room escapade throughout the hotel staff. "I am happy." She forced an energized note into her voice. "I'm just tired. I didn't sleep well last night. But everything is good."

"I hope so," Karen said, doubt lingering in her eyes. "You know, it wouldn't be a crime if you'd changed your mind about tying yourself to a mortgage. It's a lot for a young, single woman to take on. Money is going to be tight for you for a long time."

"I can handle it."

"Okay, if you say so. When it's official, I'll throw you a housewarming party."

"That sounds like fun."

As they took up their positions at the front desk, Karen added, "Maybe Cole will come back."

"I don't think so. But even if he does, it would only be for a few days to visit his aunt. Napa is not his town; it's mine."

"Sorry, Mags. I know you liked him."

"Too much," she admitted. "But I don't need a man to make me happy; I have my house." That was all she needed, wasn't it?

He was never going to sleep again, Cole decided as he got up at eight o'clock Friday morning after another sleepless night. It had been five weeks since he'd left the Stratton Hotel, and since then he'd spent three days in Mendocino, worked his way up the coast through Oregon and Washington, ending up with two weeks in the San Juan Islands. Despite the amazing views he'd encountered, he hadn't been able to get Maggie's face out of his mind.

Kicking his feet up on the coffee table, he popped open a beer and looked around his Los Angeles apartment. He'd arrived home late last night to find a fine layer of dust over everything that he owned, which wasn't much. He'd stripped down to bare essentials a few years earlier, and his apartment was as sparse and impersonal as the hotel rooms he spent most of his nights in.

He'd been happy to get rid of all his baggage—both emotional and material—to travel light, dance to his own tune, go wherever he wanted, until he'd met Maggie.

He'd missed her every second they'd been apart: her warm smile, her sparkling eyes, her crazy passion for pumpkins and pies, her genuine sense of kindness, and mostly her friendship. He didn't just miss making out with her, although he did miss that, but he missed talking to her, sharing his days with her. What the hell was wrong with him? He should have forgotten about her by now.

But as his gaze drifted to the calendar hanging on his wall, he couldn't help noticing that Thanksgiving was coming soon. Maggie had wanted to bring her family all together for that holiday, but no one had been cooperative. He hated the thought of her being alone, although she probably had her house by now, so she'd be happy about that. He just didn't know if it was enough. She thought it was, but he had his doubts.

A knock came at his door and his heart leaped into his throat. He jumped up off the couch and practically ran to the door, wondering, hoping...

His momentary excitement faded as he saw the plump, round face of his landlady. Of course it wasn't Maggie. She wouldn't be in Los Angeles. She wouldn't come to see him. She had her life, and he had his. "Hello, Mrs. Riley."

"Mr. Hastings. I saw your motorcycle in the garage and realized you were finally back."

"I returned yesterday. What can I do for you?"

"I wanted to remind you that the rent is going up two hundred dollars on the first of the month. I sent you an email about it a few weeks ago."

"I remember."

"I know you're not here very often, but the owner of the building is raising the rent on all the units. You left me a year's worth of checks, and I still have two more to go, but I'll need you to rewrite them to make up for the difference. After the first of the year, we're going to set up an electronic deposit system finally, but until then, I'll need a new check to cover December. Or if you'll be in town, you can pay me on the first."

"I'm not sure of my plans. I'll put a check in your mailbox later today.

"That will be perfect. I hope you had a good trip."

"I did."

"Must be nice to be so carefree. Sometimes I feel like I drive the same five blocks every day. You're living the dream."

"I guess I am," he said, wishing he felt more

confident in his answer. He told himself he was just tired. He'd bounce back. There were a million more places to go. The world was a big place. There was no danger of running out of new adventures. He was just beginning to wish he had someone to share those adventures with. But that definitely wasn't Maggie. Her adventures began and ended in the same city.

———❖———

"Maggie?"

Maggie started, realizing she'd been staring into space and not paying any attention to Mrs. Stratton who had stopped in front of the desk just before the end of her shift. "I'm sorry. What did you say?"

"It's my understanding that today is the big day. Antonio says you're going to hand him a check this afternoon."

"Yes, I am, just as soon as I finish my shift and get to the bank."

"Congratulations, dear. You've worked hard for this."

"Yes, I have." She noted the sparkle in Ida's eyes. "How are you and Mr. Pastorini doing?"

Ida gave her a big smile. "We're doing well. Antonio and I are going up to Lake Tahoe tomorrow morning, and we'll be staying there through the Thanksgiving holiday. Antonio has promised to cook me a turkey dinner in our own private cottage."

"That sounds lovely."

"What are you doing for the holiday—besides enjoying your new house?"

"I haven't decided yet. I may go ahead and work. Karen is scheduled, but if she has plans, and I don't, I'll take over for her."

"That's very generous. What about your family?"

"They're all gathering in Germany this year. But I'm still hoping they'll come to Napa for Christmas."

"I'd like to meet them some time."

Maggie wanted to ask her if she'd heard from Cole, and what his plans were for Thanksgiving, but she'd promised herself the day Cole left that she wouldn't pester Ida for details, not just because it was unprofessional, but because it would probably hurt worse to know more about his life than less. "Are you and Antonio going to ski? I think the mountains are getting snow later in the weekend."

"I don't ski anymore. Antonio likes to gamble, so we may play some blackjack—if we have time. We have some other things we want to do while we're there."

The sparkle in Ida's eyes put a crazy thought into Maggie's head. "You're not thinking of visiting one of those quaint wedding chapels in Tahoe, are you?"

"It's a possibility." She looked at Karen, who was busy with a guest and lowered her voice. "I'm so happy, Maggie. I never thought I'd feel this joyful again. You go through life thinking that you're just going to play out the cards you have, and then someone suddenly throws in an ace of hearts. The game changes and you're a new player. You have options you never thought you'd have."

Maggie swallowed hard. Cole had thrown some new cards into her deck, but she'd thrown them out as quickly as she could, not wanting to change her game. Had that been a mistake?

"I really have to thank you and Cole for introducing me and Antonio," Ida continued.

"I'm glad it's all worked out. I'm very happy for you

both."

"Oh, look, there's Antonio," Ida said, waving him over.

"Ida," Antonio said, love in his eyes as he placed a kiss on her cheek. Then he looked over at Maggie and smiled broadly. "Today is the big day, yes?"

"Yes. I have to deposit my paycheck first, but then I can write you a check for the down payment."

"I have the papers all ready for you to sign. We can meet whenever you're ready. If it's not today, then we'll have to do it after Thanksgiving as Ida and I have plans."

"I heard. Congratulations."

"Thank you. I love this woman more than I could ever say."

"And I love you," Ida told him.

Antonio kissed Ida without a care for who was watching. The love in their embrace sent a wave of envy through Maggie, followed by anger. She'd felt what they were feeling now, but she'd shoved that feeling away. She'd chosen a house over Cole. What the hell had she been thinking?

"What time would you like to meet to sign the papers?" Antonio asked, giving her a questioning look.

She was going to say five o'clock, but she couldn't quite get the words out.

"Maggie, is something wrong?" Ida asked, her gaze narrowing with concern.

"Yes, I think there is something wrong."

"Can I help?" Ida asked.

She shook her head. "I have to go. I have to take care of something."

"When will I see you?" Antonio asked.

She grabbed her purse out of the drawer and paused.

"I'm not sure. I'll call you later. I'll have to sign the papers after Thanksgiving."

"If that's what you want," Antonio said in surprise. "I thought you were in a hurry to put your name on the deed."

"I thought I was, too."

—————

The adrenaline pumped through Cole's body as he turned off the freeway at the Napa exit and took the highway leading into town. The sky was suddenly bluer, the grass greener, and the air sweeter. He was in Maggie country, and he couldn't wait to see her. After his landlord had asked him for new rent checks earlier in the day, he'd realized that the last thing he wanted to do was pay for an apartment in a city he didn't give a crap about. So, he'd hopped on his motorcycle and made the six-hour drive to Napa.

He wasn't sure exactly what he'd do when he got there, but he knew he was going to see Maggie, and he was going to tell her that he'd been stupid to walk away.

Hopefully, she wouldn't be the one to walk away now. He had no idea what she'd been doing since he'd left. He'd tried to get some information out of his aunt, but Ida had been oddly quiet the few times that he'd queried her, simply saying that Maggie seemed fine. For someone who'd been so eager to introduce them he found it surprising that Ida wasn't pushing for him to come back and give their relationship a chance.

Perhaps Maggie had found someone else, someone who wanted to live in Napa forever, who would move right into her house without a second thought.

He really hated the idea of another man in Maggie's

house. But if that were the case, he had no one to blame but himself. He'd been too scared and stubborn to see that what he really wanted in life had been right in front of him. Just because he'd made one mistake earlier in his life didn't have to mean he was destined to live a life of solitude. He was his own man now, and that hadn't been the case when he'd married Carole. His ex-wife was happy now with her new husband; it was time for him to move on as well, really move on—not just leave one town to go to another.

As he neared the hotel, he pushed the motorcycle to the edge of the speed limit. There was no time to waste. He'd already let too many weeks go by. He had to see Maggie now and hope it wasn't too late.

He was driving so fast down the highway that he almost missed the white Jetta on the other side of the road, the flat tire, and the woman wielding the jack. He did a double take as he passed, then immediately took the next exit. He got off the highway and then got back on again, going in the opposite direction.

He pulled up behind her and hopped off his bike, tossing his helmet to the ground.

Maggie jumped back at his approach, dropping the jack on the ground, one hand flying to her chest as he walked toward her. He pulled off his sunglasses so he could see her face, read her reaction. Right now all he saw was shock. But damn if she wasn't beautiful, with her blue eyes and reddish blonde hair, her gorgeous curves, her sweet smile. His body tightened with appreciation. She was even prettier than he remembered.

"Need some help?" he asked.

She stared at him in amazement. "Cole? What are you doing back in Napa?"

"I came to see you." He frowned, seeing the suitcases in her trunk. "Where are you going? Are you taking a trip?"

"I was going to Los Angeles."

His heart leapt into his throat. "Why?" he asked, meeting her gaze.

"To see you."

Blood pounded through his veins at her answer. *It wasn't too late.*

"I've missed you like crazy, Cole," she confessed.

"Right back at you, babe. The road has gotten really lonely since I left you. Every time I saw something interesting, I wanted to share it with you, but when I looked around, you weren't there."

"Really? You thought of me?"

"So many times." He drew in a breath, wanting to make her understand. "I thought I was happy on my own, with no one who cared about me, no one to answer to. I told myself that was real freedom, but you told me once that I'd always been free, that freedom was a choice, and you were right. I was a fool to choose the road over you. We are good together, Maggie, and I want you in my life. I need you in my life."

She licked her lips, her eyes blurring with tears. "I want you in my life, too, Cole. The last month has been hell. I've never been so unhappy, so restless. I got my paycheck today. All I had to do was put it in the bank and then write a separate check to Mr. Pastorini. He was ready to sign the house over to me, but I couldn't do it. I walked away."

He was shocked by her words. "Why? That house is what you wanted. It's what you've worked toward since you graduated from college."

"It's what I thought I wanted. But you were right, too. It's not a house I want—it's a home. It's a man. It's you. Wherever you are is where I want to be. I realize now why it didn't bother my mother to follow my father around the world, because she loved him. He was her home. And you're mine, Cole. Maybe it's crazy soon to say that. We don't know each other very well, but it's the way I feel."

"If you're crazy, so am I. I didn't think I could fall in love in a week, but I feel like I've been waiting for you my entire life."

"I feel the same, and I don't want you to worry," she added quickly. "I know you don't want a noose around your neck or a permanent address. I don't want to change you or to tie you down. I just want us to find a way to be together, wherever it makes sense for us to be. There are hotels all over the world. I can work anywhere." She let out a breath. "And now I'm going to stop talking so you can say something."

He smiled as he put his arms around her. "Don't ever stop talking, Maggie. I've missed your voice, your smile, and your mouth." He put his lips over hers in a tender, loving, possessive kiss. "I knew the first time we met you were going to change my life. That impulsive kiss was the best decision I ever made."

"I knew it, too, Cole. I just had to fight it for a while."

"I can't believe you'd give up your house for me." He felt incredibly honored by her generosity.

"The house isn't my dream anymore," she said with a simple shrug. "You are. I'm in love with you, completely and utterly in love. I was going to drive to LA to tell you that. But, of course, nothing about my life is ever easy."

He smiled as she tipped her head to the flat tire. "I'm

not sorry that tire slowed you down. Otherwise, I would have missed you, and I would have had to spend another day without you. It's not a hardship to give up my traveling for you. That's not the adventure I want anymore."

"What is the adventure you want?"

"You." He kissed her again. "You once asked me if I was running toward something, or if I was running away. The truth is that it was a little of both. Getting away from my old life was good for me. It made me see things more clearly, especially when it came to my job. But I've already learned those lessons, and the farther away I got from you, the worse I felt. Everything I wanted was in my rearview mirror."

"Would you really be happy staying in Napa?" she asked, doubt in her voice.

"I'll be happy if you're here."

"Will you need to make money again?"

"That's a yes, and I have some ideas for my future career."

"Career? That's a big word for a rambling man."

He smiled. "My aunt would like me to take over her role at the Stratton so she and Antonio can travel and do whatever they want to do."

"I saw them earlier. I think they're getting married in Tahoe this week. Did she tell you that?"

"Yeah, she mentioned something about that. I told her to wait and do it at the Stratton. She said she'd never been a patient woman."

"So you're going to be my boss, Cole? That could be a problem."

He frowned. "Really? I wouldn't be your direct boss. You'd still report to the new manager. You like her, don't you?"

"Very much. But I sort of quit my job today to come find you. So I'm not sure I'm working there anymore."

A smile curved his lips. "I think you can get your job back."

"Do you really want to run a hotel?"

"It is the family business. But I do have some thoughts beyond overseeing the Stratton."

"Like what?"

"Like maybe building a smaller boutique hotel on the grounds of a winery."

Her eyes sparkled. "That would be cool."

"Would you want to help me?"

"I would be happy to. How exciting would that be?"

"My thought exactly. I know we're moving fast, but I want to make something really clear. I'm all in with you, Maggie. I want the house, the marriage, the kids, everything. I want to be tied to you in every possible way. I have no fear of commitment as long as I'm committing to you."

"That's an amazing thing to say. I don't want you to change your whole life. We can compromise. I want you to be happy, too."

"We'll both be happy. I love you, Maggie."

"I love you, Cole."

He kissed her again and then said the words that he'd never thought he'd say again. "Take me home, babe."

Epilogue

Three weeks later

The yard behind an old church on a hillside overlooking the Pacific Ocean in the charming town of Half Moon Bay was the site of Julie's wedding. Maggie stood in the line of bridesmaids as Julie and Matt vowed their love to each other. She was touched by the look of adoration in Matt's eyes as he gazed at his bride, and she'd never seen Julie look happier. As emotion filled her heart, her gaze drifted to Cole, who was sitting in one of the white folding chairs in the last row.

He looked so handsome in his dark suit and red tie, brown hair styled, his face freshly shaven. He was still her bad boy, but she'd begun to realize that he had a lot more going for him than just a sexy swagger. He was incredibly smart, organized, and determined, and in three short weeks, he'd made significant changes at the Stratton and also in his own life.

He'd moved into her house for one, and he'd also bought some land in the valley to build a boutique hotel and winery, and they'd spent hours talking about what kind of hotel they would build and what kind of wine they would make. For a man who had once been happy to travel the open road with just a duffel bag, Cole was now ready to take on the role of being a landowner, a homeowner, a business owner, and some day in the not so distant future—a husband and a father.

She was happy to share a new dream with Cole, a dream that was so much better than her last one. Although she had officially purchased her home, and Cole had insisted she put the deed in her name only, the accomplishment was not what she had envisioned. She still loved the house, but she loved Cole more. She'd probably sell the house once they got married, once they built a life for themselves together, but that was down the road. Right now, she was happy to share her house with the only man she'd ever really loved.

She turned her attention back to the bride and groom as the minister announced their new union to the crowd.

Julie and Matt then walked down the aisle, the bridesmaids and ushers following behind.

"She did it," Jessica said to Maggie, as they watched Julie and Matt pose for more pictures while the guests began to move toward the meeting room next to the church where they would be treated to a catered dinner.

"It was beautiful," Maggie said. "I liked that the guest list was small. It feels intimate, and that's what Julie wanted."

"It was perfect. She and Matt lead a big life; this day was just for them, and us, of course."

Maggie thought she heard an odd note in Jessica's voice. "Everything okay?"

"Oh, sure, just feeling emotional. Weddings can be happy and sometimes a little sad for me."

"You'll find the right man for you, Jess. I know it."

"I thought I had the right man before, but I didn't."

"You were twenty-one years old. Next time will be different."

"Next time I'll have to be even more careful; I have Brandon now. I have to make sure I don't just pick a good husband but also a good father."

"I know you will," she said confidently.

"So, has Cole asked you to marry him yet?"

"Not yet, but I think we're headed that way."

Jessica smiled. "Well, get in line, honey. We still have Isabella's wedding in the spring, so unless you two want to double up, you better push any wedding dates back to next summer. Thank goodness, I'm going to be living here soon. It's hard to keep up with all the parties."

"We're happy you're going to be closer, too, and I would love a summer wedding in Napa. But Cole and I are not in a rush. We're just really enjoying each other."

"It's great to see you so happy, Maggie. And here we all thought it was only a house that could make your eyes sparkle like that."

She laughed. "I did get a little crazy about that house."

"What's this I hear about you getting crazy?" Cole interrupted, sliding his arm around her waist as he kissed her cheek. "Are you talking about being crazy for me?"

"I was talking about the house," she said, meeting his teasing gaze. "But I am crazy for you, too."

Jessica laughed. "I think that's my cue to leave you two alone."

"You don't have to go," Cole said. "I didn't mean to interrupt."

"You didn't. It's all good. I'll catch up with you both at the reception."

"Is she okay?" Cole asked, a thoughtful gleam in his eyes.

"She gets a little sad at weddings, but she'll be all right. We'll make sure of it."

"Before you join the others, there is something I want to talk to you about, Maggie. You've been really busy lately, and I know you haven't had time to think about Christmas, but I have an idea."

"What's that?"

He pulled out what appeared to be two airplane tickets. "I think we should go somewhere for the holiday."

"Well, we did talk about spending Christmas with your parents when we saw them last weekend, but I didn't know that was final."

"It's not. My parents are actually going to Hawaii for Christmas. We are going to Germany."

Her heart skipped a beat, and she was both excited and unsure of his plan. "Really?"

"You've been wanting a holiday family dinner. If they won't come to you, I say we go to them."

"But that wasn't the point."

"The point was to be together."

She sighed. "You're not going to let me be stubborn about it, are you?"

"No, because I think you need to be with your family. I know you missed them at Thanksgiving, and it doesn't matter where the next holiday happens; it just matters that you're together. If you don't want me to go with you—"

"Don't be ridiculous. Of course you're coming with me. I just hope you're ready to meet my father. He can be very much the Army general."

Cole tipped his head. "I can take whatever he dishes out as long as he gives me the right answer to one question."

"What's that?"

"I want to ask him if I can have the hand of his daughter in marriage."

She looked into his eyes and her heart overflowed with love. "Don't you think you should ask his daughter first?"

He smiled. "In this case, I think I might win more points if I went straight to your dad. He seems like the kind of man who likes tradition."

"You're right. He is." She paused. "Just so you know, Cole, when you do want to ask me, I'm going to say yes."

"What a relief," he said with a laugh. "Now go be a bridesmaid. I'll be waiting for you when you're done. We're going to dance the night away."

"I like the sound of that. I love you, Cole."

"I love you back, Maggie. Now and forever."

"I only hope that's long enough."

THE END

The next book in the
Bridesmaids and Batchelors Series:

FOREVER STARTS TONIGHT

will be released in 2016

—————⟫⟪⟫⟨⟨—————

Keep on reading for an excerpt from

BEAUTIFUL STORM

Book #1 in Barbara's new

Lightning Strikes Trilogy

Excerpt – BEAUTIFUL STORM

(Lightning Strikes Trilogy #1)
© Copyright 2015 Barbara Freethy
All Rights Reserved

One

The clouds had been blowing in off the ocean for the last hour, an ominous foreboding of the late September storm moving up the Miami coast. It was just past five o'clock in the afternoon, but the sky was dark as night.

Alicia Monroe drove across Florida's Rickenbacker Causeway toward Virginia Key Park, located on the island of Key Biscayne. Most of the traffic moved in the opposite direction as the island had a tendency to flood during fierce storms. According to the National Weather Service, the storm would bring at least six inches of rain plus high winds, thunder and lightning.

Alicia pressed her foot down harder on the gas. As her tires skidded on the already damp pavement, a voice inside her head told her to slow down, that a picture wasn't worth her life, but the adrenaline charging through her body made slowing down impossible.

She'd been obsessed with electrical storms all her life. She'd grown up hearing her Mayan great-grandmother speak of lightning gods. Her father had also told her tales about the incredible blue balls of fire and red flaming sprites he'd witnessed while flying for the Navy and later as a civilian pilot.

Their stories had enthralled her, but they'd been an embarrassment to the rest of the family, especially when her father had begun to tell his stories outside the family. Neither her mother nor her siblings had appreciated the fact that a former Navy hero was now being referred to as *Lightning Man.*

A wave of pain ran through her at the memories of her father and the foolish nickname that had foreshadowed her dad's tragic death years later in a fierce electrical storm.

She'd been sixteen years old when he'd taken his last flight. It was supposed to be a typical charter run to drop a hunting party in the mountains and then return home, but after dropping the men at their destination, her father's plane had run into a massive storm. When the rain stopped and the sun came back out, there was no sign of her father or his plane. He'd quite simply disappeared somewhere over the Gulf of Mexico.

Everyone assumed he'd crashed. They'd sent out search parties to find him or at least pieces of the plane, but those searches had returned absolutely nothing. How a man and a small plane could completely vanish seemed impossible to accept, and she'd spent years trying to find an answer, but so far that hadn't happened.

What had happened was her increasingly obsessive fascination with storm photography.

Her sister Danielle thought she was looking for her dad in every flash of lightning. Her brother Jake thought she was crazy, and her mother Joanna just wanted her to stop challenging Mother Nature by running headlong into dangerous storms. But like her dad, Alicia didn't run away from storms; she ran toward them.

While she worked as a photojournalist for the *Miami Chronicle* to pay the rent, her true passion was taking photographs of lightning storms and displaying them on her website and in a local art gallery.

It was possible that she was looking for the truth about her dad's disappearance in the lightning, or that she just had a screw loose. It was also possible that she was tempting fate by her constant pursuit of dangerous storms, but even if that was all true, she couldn't stop, not yet, not until she knew…something. She just wasn't sure what that *something* was.

Her cell phone rang through her car, yanking her mind back to reality. "Hello?"

"Where are you?" Jeff Barkley asked.

"Almost to the park." Jeff was the weather reporter at the local television station and had become her best resource for storm chasing.

"Turn around, Alicia. The National Weather Service is predicting the possibility of a ten-to-fifteen-foot storm surge, which would make the causeway impassable, and you'll be stranded on the island."

"I'll get the lightning shots before that happens. How's the storm shaping up?"

"Severe thunderstorms predicted."

"Great."

"It's not great, Alicia."

"You know what I mean," she grumbled. She didn't

wish ill on anyone. But the more magnificent the storm, the better her pictures would be.

"You keep pushing the limits. One of these days, you'll go too far," Jeff warned.

"That won't be today. It's barely drizzling yet. The island is the perfect place to capture the storm in two places—over the ocean and then as it passes over Miami. Don't worry, I'll be fine."

"You always say that."

"And it's always true."

"So far. Text me when you get back."

"I will."

Ending the call, she drove into the parking lot. The attendant booth was closed, and a sign said the park was closed, but there was no barrier to prevent her from entering the lot.

She parked as close as she could to the trail leading into the park. She'd no sooner shut down the engine and turned off her headlights when lightning lit up the sky. She rolled down her window and took a few quick shots with her digital camera. She didn't have a great angle, so she would definitely have to find a higher point in the park to get a better picture.

Putting her digital camera on the console, she grabbed her waterproof backpack that held her more expensive film camera and got out of the car.

The force of the wind whipped her long, brown ponytail around her face. She pulled the hood of her raincoat over her head. It was just misting at the moment, but the sky would be opening up very soon. With tall rain boots and a long coat to protect her jeans and knit shirt, she was protected from the elements, not that she worried much about getting wet. She was more concerned with keeping her equipment dry until she needed to use it.

This was her second trip to the island, so she knew exactly which path to take, and she headed quickly in that direction. While the trails were popular with walkers, hikers, and bikers on most days, there wasn't another soul in sight. Anyone with any sense had left the park to seek shelter.

She was used to shooting storms in dark, shadowy places, but for some reason her nerves were tighter than usual today. The air was thick, almost crackling, and the atmosphere was dark and eerie. She felt a little spooked, as if someone were watching her.

A crash in the trees behind her brought her head around, and her heart skipped a beat at the dancing shadows behind her.

A second later, she saw two raccoons scurry into the woods, and she blew out a breath of relief. The animals were just looking for shelter. Everything was fine.

Ten minutes of a rapid jog had her heart pounding and her breath coming fast as she traversed the hilly section of the park, finally reaching the clearing at the top of the trail. Instead of thick brush and trees, she was now looking at the churning waves of the Atlantic Ocean. But it wasn't the sea that sent a nervous shiver down her spine; it was the towering, tall clouds that the meteorologists called cumulonimbus clouds. These clouds were associated with thunder and lightning storms and atmospheric instability. Alicia felt both terrified and entranced by the potential fury of the stormy sky.

She pulled out her film camera. While digital more often these days, there was still nothing like capturing a storm on film.

She took several quick consecutive shots as lightning

cracked over the ocean. She checked her watch, noting the lapse of fifteen seconds before the thunder boomed. That meant the lightning was about three miles away.

Eight seconds later, lightning split apart the clouds, jagged bolts heading toward the beach. The storm was moving in fast—the lightning less than a mile away now.

She had a feeling she knew where it would strike next.

Dashing down the adjacent trail, she headed toward the old carousel with the shiny gold decorative rods that would more than likely attract the lightning.

As she moved through the thick brush, the rain began to come down harder, but she didn't slow her pace. She just wiped the water from her eyes and kept going.

When lightning lit up the park in front of her, she raised her camera and snapped two more photos before venturing farther down the trail. The carousel was just ahead.

The thunder was so loud it almost knocked her off of her feet.

She stopped abruptly as another jagged streak of lightning hit the carousel, illuminating the area around it. Captured in the glaringly bright light were a man and a woman engaged in a struggle.

The man raised his hand, something metal glinting between his fingers. A knife?

The woman screamed.

Alicia took a step forward, but the light disappeared and everything was dark again. She juggled her phone, trying to turn on the flashlight so she could see where to go.

Another boom of thunder.

Another flash of lightning.

She saw more dancing shadows. Then heard a long, penetrating scream. Closer now. The woman seemed to be running toward her.

She needed to help her. She moved down the path, stumbling over some rocks, and then the lightning came again. The tree next to her exploded from the strike. A heavy branch flew through the air, knocking her flat on the ground. She hit her head on a rock, feeling a flash of pain that threatened to take her under.

She battled against the feeling, knowing she had to get away from the fire that was crackling around her.

Where the hell was the rain now?

It was still coming down but not enough to smother the fire.

She got to her feet, ruthlessly fighting her way through the flaming branches.

Finally, the skies opened up, and the rain poured down, putting out the fire and allowing her to get free.

She grabbed her backpack from under a branch and moved down the trail.

Using her flashlight again, she walked toward the carousel, her tension increasing with each step, but there was no one around. No man, no woman, no knife, no struggle. What the hell had happened? Where had they gone?

She looked around in bewilderment. It had only been a few minutes since she'd seen them—hadn't it? Or had she lost consciousness when the tree had knocked her down?

She didn't think so, but her mind felt hazy and her head ached.

Despite the fuzzy feeling, she couldn't forget the image of the tall man towering over the smaller woman.

She could still hear the woman's scream of terror in her head.

She turned slowly around, seeing nothing of significance in the shadowy surroundings. Then something in the dirt brought her gaze to the ground. She squatted down and picked up a shiny, rectangular military ID tag.

Her stomach turned over. She had a tag just like this in her jewelry box at home, the tag that had belonged to her father.

But it wasn't her father's name on this tag; it was a woman's name: Liliana Valdez, United States Navy, blood type O positive, religion Catholic. Her birth date indicated that she was twenty-eight.

The name didn't mean anything to Alicia, but she still felt an odd connection to the woman who'd lost it. Had it been the woman she'd seen fighting for her life? Had that woman been wearing a uniform?

She couldn't remember. She had the sense that the woman had worn a long, dark coat, but the details escaped her. Maybe she'd caught them on film. That thought took her to her feet.

She needed to get home and develop the photographs. She walked quickly back to the parking lot, pausing for just a moment to get a few more shots of the lightning now streaking across the Miami skyline.

Then she got into her car and sped toward the causeway, hoping she hadn't waited too long to cross before the storm surge made the bridge impassable.

When she reached the bridge, water was splashing over the rail, but she made it back to Miami without incident. She felt relieved to be in the city, but the pain in her temple reminded her of what she'd seen by the carousel. Who were those people? Had something terrible happened? Had she been a witness to…what?

Alicia's gaze dropped to the ID tag sitting on her console—to the name Liliana Valdez. She needed to find Liliana; not just to return her tag but also to make sure she was all right, that she was still alive.

———

Alicia lived in the Wynwood Art District, a neighborhood just north of downtown Miami and known for its art galleries, boutiques and charming cafés. She lived on the second floor of a two-story building, and the bottom floor housed the art gallery where she displayed her storm photographs.

The owner of Peterman Art Gallery, Eileen Peterman, had leased her the apartment a year earlier, and Alicia was happy to be close to the gallery and in a neighborhood filled with artists and designers. She'd always been more comfortable among creative people who thought outside of the box, colored beyond the lines, and who put their emotions on display, whether it be in a sculpture or a painting or a photograph. She'd never been able to trust anyone who hid their emotions. It always made her wonder what else they were hiding.

After entering her apartment, Alicia dropped her backpack on the floor, set her keys and the ID tag on the side table, and then took off her wet raincoat and hung it on a hook by the door. She kicked off her boots and walked into the bathroom to grab a towel.

After drying her face, she pulled out the band from her hair and ran the blow-dryer through the damp dark tangles of her unruly mass of dark brown waves. Her hair was thick and long, drifting past her shoulder blades, and it was a constant battle to straighten the rebellious curls, which had gotten more out of hand in the wind and the rain.

As she stared at her face in the mirror, she was a little surprised at the size of the bump on her throbbing forehead. It was turning a lovely shade of purple and black and definitely stood out against her unusually pale skin. A dark-eyed brunette with olive skin, she usually had a vibrant, exotic look about her, but today was not one of those days. What little makeup she'd put on earlier that day had washed away in the rain, and the pain of her aching head injury had put strained lines around her eyes.

She set down the dryer, grabbed some ibuprofen from the medicine cabinet, took two capsules, and told herself she'd feel a lot better in about thirty minutes. Then she walked back to the living room.

She picked up Liliana's ID tag and took it over to the kitchen table. Opening her laptop computer, she typed in Liliana's name, age, and birth date. The Valdez surname would be common in Miami, a city made up of thousands of Cuban and Puerto Rican immigrants, so she was expecting her search to be complicated and long.

Surprisingly, it was neither.

The headline of the first article jumped off the page: *JAG attorney missing in Miami.*

As she read through the news story, she discovered that Liliana Valdez, a Navy lieutenant and attorney with the Judge Advocate General, had gone missing while visiting Miami in late July for the wedding of her sister. She'd last been seen in the parking lot outside of Paladar, a popular Cuban restaurant in Little Havana. The vehicle she'd been driving had been recovered from the parking lot, but there was no sign of a struggle or any other clues to her whereabouts.

Alicia let out a breath and sat back on the couch, staring out the window where rain now streamed against the panes.

Liliana Valdez had disappeared two months ago, and no one had seen her since.

Alicia picked up the ID tag, still a little damp and gritty with dirt, and ran her fingers over Liliana's name, feeling the same sense of connection she'd felt earlier.

She had a clue to a missing woman. She needed to take it to the police.

Jumping to her feet, she paused, struck by the thought that she might have more than one clue. Retrieving her camera, she took it into the walk-in closet off her bedroom that she'd turned into her personal darkroom.

Unfortunately, as the pictures developed, Alicia's enthusiasm began to fade.

The couple she'd seen by the carousel did not appear in any of the shots. The lightning was spectacular, but it was so close, so bright, it was impossible to see anything but shadows beyond the light, certainly nothing that clearly defined a person, which meant she had no other clue besides the military tag. Still, it was something. Hopefully, it would be enough to help find the missing woman.

END OF EXCERPT

About The Author

Barbara Freethy is a #1 New York Times Bestselling Author of 45 novels ranging from contemporary romance to romantic suspense and women's fiction. Traditionally published for many years, Barbara opened her own publishing company in 2011 and has since sold over 5 million books! Twenty of her titles have appeared on the New York Times and USA Today Bestseller Lists.

Known for her emotional and compelling stories of love, family, mystery and romance, Barbara enjoys writing about ordinary people caught up in extraordinary adventures. Barbara's books have won numerous awards. She is a six-time finalist for the RITA for best contemporary romance from Romance Writers of America and a two-time winner for DANIEL'S GIFT and THE WAY BACK HOME.

Barbara has lived all over the state of California and currently resides in Northern California where she draws much of her inspiration from the beautiful bay area.

For a complete listing of books, as well as excerpts and contests, and to connect with Barbara:

Visit Barbara's Website:
www.barbarafreethy.com

Join Barbara on Facebook:
www.facebook.com/barbarafreethybooks

Follow Barbara on Twitter:
www.twitter.com/barbarafreethy

51734548R00125

Made in the USA
San Bernardino, CA
01 August 2017